THE Midnight Fish & OTHER STORIES

Scott Bowen

International Standard Book Number (ISBN): 0970547501
Library of Congress Control Number: 2001087769

The Morris-Lee
Publishing Group

Cane Farm • Bldg. 11 • Route 519
P.O. Box 218
Rosemont, NJ 08556-0218
609 397-8538 • 609 397-9275 (fax)
e-mail: morris04@sprynet.com

CONTENTS

This book is dedicated to my family.

Many thanks to Keen Butterworth, Ben Greer, Bill Fox, and Jim Dickey. Thanks to Jim Morris-Lee. Thanks to anyone who ever showed me places to fish. Thanks to dad who often took me to those places.

Thank you to all the fish.

INTRODUCTION

At the time of the writing of these stories, I was asked a routine question from a group of friends who don't fish: How do you know what to catch a fish with? I gave a pat answer; actually a ridiculous answer. You have to think like a fish, I said.

This is an unfortunate anthropomorphism that I am afraid these friends of mine now believe. Gamefish are not people, though they come in as great a variety as people, down to the individual. But "thinking like a fish" is an impossibility that suggests that fish have reason, which they do not, otherwise they would be people; and "thinking like a fish" also implies that anglers actually think at all.

Okay, anglers do think. But I have never truly felt that I have "out thought" a fish, though I may have created some characters here who believe they can. More accurately, I use an artificial means—a fly or a plug—to enter into a fish's environment in an act of deception. I place myself upon a body of water as close to a fish's lair as possible. I consider the water, the weather, and what the fish may be eating, and attempt to get as close as I can to the perfect charade.

This voluntary attempt takes an angler to a place that is riddled with traps and pitfalls. Within this world, you can do things exactly right, and do other things totally wrong, yet still be the same person—foolish and brilliant all at once. You decorate trees with flies and spinners. You yank lures away from fish just as they bite. You can fish ineptly, however, and still catch great fish. You can also be almost perfect with casts, timing, and fly selection, and go crazy with fishlessness, then come home and, forced by honesty or guilt, tell the truth and say you once again caught nothing.

Yes, anglers do tell the truth, more often than not, I find. You risk your credibility with too many consecutive tales of dozens of catches. There are some people who anglers absolutely cannot lie to and those people are usually other, respected anglers. For the rest of the public, anglers don't need to go into details. There is no statute of limitations on piscatorial records when talking to non-anglers, so those bass and trout that were caught six months ago work fine when someone asks at a party, "Hey, how's the fishing?" and you have been flogging the water fruitlessly for three days, having realized a fishing vest is a kind of straight jacket.

The luck and thrill of pursuing and engaging gamefish are what make me go out on the water, and later reflect imaginatively on doing so. And then there is folly, always folly, which has its perverse attractions too.

This is the answer I give when friends ask, "Why do you fish? Why write about it?" I can try to give better explanations, of course, and will very quickly sound like some person on a talk show getting deeper and deeper into psycho-blather and literary pompishness. I can state only that I learn great deal from coping with things that go wrong in big and small ways (folly); that I utterly believe in rhythms of chance beyond pure physics (luck); and that nothing compares to a good fish fighting (thrill). These things call upon me to consider them in writing.

There is no fun in a thorough understanding of any subject. A domain that naturally contains more mystery than is solvable on any given day, like fishing, is very enjoyable. Such mystery overflows itself. The want to go fishing and the effects of fishing change people's lives. The folly, luck, and thrill stay with you after you leave the water and resonate in other aspects of your life, commingling with the folly of one's suit-and-tie career, the luck of turning your head in the right direction at the right moment, and the thrill of the best-laid plans bringing unexpected results. These are the essential themes of these stories.

Beyond the philosophical and literary factors, there is everything else of fishing: The sound of people's voices made by a running stream. Diving ospreys. The motion of a snake swimming across a pond. The smell of the sea and the colors of a fading night sky, and the edge of the sunrise on the horizon. Fishing alone then laughing with others around a fire. Sitting on a rock in the middle of a river, watching the river change colors at sundown. Rain after a hot day. Having secret places.

Scott Bowen
January 2001

ONE

River Solstice

The first moon of summer, full and
As red as Mars, eases atop
The tall black trees while the wide
River changes—dark green   brown   blue.

Wading barelegged I cast to black
Swirls—there—a fish takes the white
Streamer, runs, jumps three times, a wet
Ingot popping from the forge.

I reel him in, catch him in the net.
Small, eight inches maybe, bronze back
And stripes clear in the azure light
Between moon and river; his eyes

A dark blood brown, belly white.
A strong, fast little fish. I put
Him back. Wobbly, he floats, finds his
Senses.   He is gone.   Now darkness:

Land water sky: one blue layer
Under the moon. I walk slowly
Through the river, casting, immersed
Again in cool, weightless night.

Two

The Lost Striper

The big fish hit the Deceiver in the swells and raced down the beach. Joe stood in the breakers in his chest waders, the rod high over him like an archer's bow. I listened to the singing of the line running out. I wondered if the fish was able to run down the entire spool. We had never seen a fish do that.

I was sitting on the beach watching the sun come up over the ocean when the fish hit. I sat on the sand with my rod across my legs. I nodded with the waves, half asleep, my eyes swollen from the salty air. Then I had heard Joe shout, looked up, and saw him whip his rod around in an arc. He reeled once, hard, then the drag buzzed. He had no line in his basket; the fish hit at the top of his cast. As I stood I saw a swirl of foam not far away but did not see how big the fish was. Joe's rod turned in his hands and he nearly toppled as he swiveled his body. He put the rod over his head and the line buzzed. Not far out in the slick blue water his fish steadily moved away. This was a big striper.

I watched Joe trot through the rolling breakers, foam washing around his stout legs and splashing up into his arm pits. He kept the rod up and watched the reel. I watched him for a few minutes and counted, one-thousand-one, one-thousand-two. When I got to eleven thousand-one I got up and jogged in Joe's direction. I enjoy helping someone land a fish as much as I enjoy catching my own. I remembered Joe's predawn remark that his reel did not have as much backing as it should, one of those stupid flaws in your fishing that you idly notice. He had a nice, old Pate reel and it looked all right to me.

Joe left the water and jogged down the wet sand. I saw him go: a stout, pepper-and-gray haired man ungainly in his waders.

It was six-thirty in the morning. Few other anglers were on the beach. The October sun sat round and yellow over the ocean. The sky was hazy around the sun, pale blue above, then turned indigo over my head and behind me. The ocean was black-blue and rolly.

I slogged through the gray Jersey sand, my feet clumsy in the boots. A fisherman running in his waders appears like a very big bird trying to get up speed to take off.

Joe was back out in the water where the waves sloshed up to fringed white ridges. The waves rode up under the armpits of his jacket then tipped over in a curl and the foam spread behind him. The fish had turned for deeper water and was running diagonally away from the beach. Maybe this was Joe's lifetime catch. When I came up beside him in the cold water I shouted, How much line have you got?

Not much, he said.

I looked at his reel. I saw a solid but thin layer of backing. He looked at me with a slightly embarrassed expression. I said, I've got a spool of braided line in my jacket. Think I could tie it on?

Joe said he wanted to back up. The waves were cresting his waders. The breakers weren't rough, just fat, careening belts of water that tipped over at the last second. He steadily reeled in line as we walked backward through the foam. I imagined the fish out there: a green, gold, and black torpedo. Friends of mine tell me trout are the most beautiful fish. Trout probably are, but I don't think my friends have seen a nice striper flash inside a rising wave, in the sun, like a slab of gold and emerald.

I had never tied on more backing before and neither had Joe. This idea was also probably illegal, or at least against somebody's book of rules. But we both knew a striper as big as this—one that had shown such power as this—could easily take his whole spool.

What do you think? I said.

He's going to run again, Joe said and as he said this the rod nodded and line went out again. The fish ran him down to what looked like twenty wraps of backing. Then Joe began to gain line back. The fish was out there, I mean out there. I began to wonder if this was a striper at all; if a shark or something else, a big eel maybe, had hit the fly.

Joe looked at me. He said, Can you do it?

Yeah, I said. The wind was slight but awful. I got on my knees in the wash of the breakers and blocked the wind with my back. Joe clamped the running line with his fingers and stripped all the backing off the reel, letting it fall on me and I cut it. I focused on my fingers and worked quickly despite how cold and clumsy my fingers were: backing bound to braided line in a lumpy surgeon's knot.

I payed out the black cloth line from the spool, letting it fly in the air. Joe let it slip through his fingers. I stripped coils and coils off the plastic spool and when I thought I had as much as I dared I cut it and tied it to Joe's spool, then wound the reel as he tendered the line with his hands. Had anyone seen us, they would have thought us mad. Joe let the line slide through his fingers, letting the rod do the work as the striper, mercifully, swam slowly, as if readying to up the ante.

The fish ran out some more line, well into the black line, then it just held down in the water. Joe tugged back and forth with the fish for ten minutes.

As the sun rose Joe began to gain line. The fish was tiring. Joe fell silent then, and his arms got jerky. That's how he gets when he's got a big one on the line: quiet, his arms nervous. Big stripers give him a buzz and unsettle him a little too the way a good thrill should.

Slowly, as the sun filled the morning sky and the sky itself became a perfect blue, Joe gained line on the fish. I watched the cirrus clouds smear like icing way high up and watched Joe labor in the breakers as he brought the fish in. He slowly walked back along the sand the way we came. There's a hole here somewhere, he said. I want to get past it. It's nice and flat on the other side. He kept walking. Then we both went out in the water, our numbed, clumsy feet digging in the flat of ridged sand.

The sun shone from high enough that we were able to see a little into the water, the ocean changing color as the morning and tide progressed. We saw the line but no fish yet in the green-blue. The problem now was that the reel was over-filled so the coils bulged and began to catch on the seat housing. Joe stripped line into the basket around his waist where it coiled like cold spaghetti.

I went a little further out with the boga grip in my hands. I watched the line and saw a golden mote not far away. There it was, the big striper. I waited to see the fish break the surface.

As the line twanged over my shoulder I saw something else out there. I shook my head with cold. Water had run down the insides of my waders. I couldn't feel my toes. My sides shook with cold, and my ears were numb. I was sure, though, that my vision was not affected: I had seen something very big rise against the surface tension of a slack wave.

Then I saw it, the image we all have in our heads: a shark's dorsal fin. It rose gently out of the water and moved slowly. The tip of the tail fin sliced the water behind.

For a second I wasn't able to move. This was a big shark. No sand shark either. A bull maybe, or a dusky. The dorsal fin was very sharp and stout.

I called to Joe, Reel in! I didn't know if he had seen the shark but I heard him strip line and curse. I began to back out of the water, the swells rising just along the top of my waders. Faster, I shouted.

I looked back at Joe. His expression was panicked but I didn't know if that was because of the fight or because he had seen the shark. He rode the waves, rod up, yanking the line. As I turned back to the ocean I saw the whole thing just as Joe saw it.

The striper rose on the surface. We saw its broad green back and its bodily glow beneath. It was massive, unbelievable. I heard Joe call out, Oh, please.

From the side the shark eased toward the poor striper, taking its time, then it turned with a flinch and speared the tired bass. Its tail fin whipped and powered it on. In the cut-away of a rising wave I saw the whole shark as its broad body bulged out of the wave. I saw the sharp nose, the corner of its mouth and its big round, black eye. A mako.

The shark thrashed and sent up a cascade of foam. Then it disappeared. Joe was still stripping line and cried out curses and undecipherable sounds of protest and anguish. We backed up the beach and stood in silence as Joe pulled in the gory head of a trophy striper.

For a long time we stood and looked at it. It was horrible. The striper had been bitten off just behind its gill covers. The striper's jaws and gills jerked reflexively as if it still wasn't giving up. Its blood made maroon puddles on the wet sand.

Joe sat down on the sand and closed his eyes. I didn't want to say anything so I just sighed. There was nothing to say anyway.

We fished all day, not talking, and caught nothing. The day was sunny and cold. We decided to go home.

Driving down the road before we came to the bridge over the bay I asked Joe to pull into a bait shack, not Betty and Nick's place, because I didn't want people in-the-know to see what I was going to do. I told Joe I wanted to get some soda. I went to the trunk and took the striper head out of the garbage bag where I had hidden it. Joe had thrown it into the dunes, but I went and got it when he had gone to pee somewhere.

I tucked the bag under my anorak and went in the shack while Joe waited behind the wheel. His face was slack. He stared straight ahead.

Inside the shack some thick-necked local men were standing around the counter talking to the heavy-set owner. I went to them and took the striper head out of the bag. Their eyes widened. The shack owner said, What the hell happened with that?

Shark came up in the surf and ate it. What's this weigh?

The man took the head from me and put it on the scale. From nose to gills the striper weighed roughly eight pounds. The men whistled. You might've had a record there, man, one of them said. I shrugged. I bought a bottle of Gatorade and walked out, the sand-covered fish head sitting on the scale behind me, the three big guys standing there looking at it.

When I sat on the seat Joe didn't start the car. He said, How much did it weigh?

You really want to know?

He looked through the windshield for a moment. He hiccoughed. He said, All right, tell me, but before I got out a word he said, No, no, don't tell me.

I didn't tell him. After ten years, neither one of us has ever said a word.

THREE

Jake's Arm

Uncle Jake came and went unannounced, staying a few days then leaving. His arrivals chagrined my mother. She seemed more distracted than angry to have him around the house. She called him a "bum" once or twice after he left. She thought he was a bum, I supposed, because he had managed to make three wives all leave him. He didn't have to pay alimony that way, he said, though he had lost half his possessions three times, so he was one-hundred-fifty percent in the hole. He always got on with his life, whatever it was. I once heard my father say to him, kidding, Jake, marry a rich woman this time. My mother's eyes flared from across the dinner table. Uncle Jake considered my father's advice and replied, I have been thinking the same thing.

Jake never had the same job each time we saw him, usually in the late spring when he arrived to go fishing where he grew up. He appeared in our driveway, each time with a different used car. He and my father sat on the patio and had scotch on the rocks—my mother also thought Jake was a bad influence on my innocent father—and Jake explained what he was doing for money that particular year. The last three jobs Jake had, that I can remember, were assistant store manager of an A&P, a salesman for a car parts company, and some sort of position with the Republican Party.

When she first saw him in the driveway, or standing in the living room, mom glanced at the floor as if embarrassed, then went up and hugged him, kissed his cheek, and asked him how he was. He treated her genuinely nice and called her "Peggie." He was always well mannered, though he slept late when he could and mom did not like that. He took food and beer from our refrigerator as if it were his and he always replaced everything before he left. My father didn't mind having him around. After all, Jake was my mother's brother, and dad actually liked the guy. But muggy air settled between mom and dad while Jake was in the house. They didn't fight or not talk to each other, but dad behaved carefully lest he screw up and become categorized with his brother-in-law.

One time I caught my mother looking at Jake and she seemed about to cry. Another time I caught her looking at him as if he had once done her a terrible wrong. Later I asked her, Don't you like him? and she said quickly, Of course I do. Only a couple of times did she ever get angry with him, talking at him sharply about his last two wives leaving him. Perhaps she hoped marriage was his only chance of straightening out his life.

And only once did she ask him to leave. Some neighbors had come over for a cookout, bringing a college-aged daughter with them. Jake got this girl a little drunk, himself a little drunk, and the girl's father found them kissing behind the garage. She told him, Leave, and he packed his bags and drove away the same night without protest.

Jake looked nothing like his sister. Mom had reddish-brown hair and amber eyes. My father told me over and over how he thought she looked like a skinny Ann

Margaret when he was dating her. Dad obviously had wanted to date Ann Margaret.

Jake had wavy blond hair that was dark at the roots, and he had blue eyes of a watery, lapis blue. His nose and his lips were thin. He was tall and lean but had a muscular neck with a sharp Adam's apple, and he had a sinewy arm. Just one.

Jake's left arm stopped mid-bicep, and the false arm attached there. The prosthesis was the most amazing thing I had ever seen. Jake told me he had it made in Switzerland because that was the only country in the world where things were made properly. But another time he said he had it made in Germany, so I suspected he had it made in New Jersey, where we lived, by someone who was very good at making such things.

The forearm was made from solid but light-weight, blackened wood like the wood billy clubs were made of. At the upper end of the forearm was a ratcheting ball-and-socket joint made of blue-blacked steel gears connected to a thick wooden cap that formed the upper portion. Jake used this joint as his elbow, able to swing his arm up a few clicks then rotate it inward or outward. To lower his arm he had to pull it by the wrist with his other hand to free the gear teeth and let it down. The cuff that attached the whole thing to his stump was made of black rubber that fit tightly and was cinched by a thin black nylon belt. At the other end, the hand was made of heavy, malleable rubber so that it could be shaped into various forms. One of the funniest things I ever saw was how Jake once very quickly dropped the arm straight, fiddled with the rubber fingers, then flinched and swung the black arm up *chat-chat-chat-chat* so his long black middle finger pointed straight up. He and I laughed and laughed.

I had begged my mother to let me go fishing with Jake

but she never relented. She was unable to prevent her wastrel brother from coming and staying a few days, and she was unable to prevent her husband from liking him, but she was going to keep her son away from the bum.

One early summer Jake arrived in the late afternoon while mom and dad and my sister were at the swim club. Jake easily made himself at home with a beer and a sandwich, sitting in the living room watching golf. I sat with him. He said, You know, Len, I always wanted to play golf. I always wanted to be good at that because I think I could have made some money.

You think you could have played on one of the tours? I said.

No. I think maybe I could have worked myself up to semi-pro, maybe, but then gambled on it. Lots of guys like to gamble on their golf game. I'd just have to be better than them. But with this—he swung the arm up, a cigarette tucked between the rubber fingers—I've got no feel on the club. I tried, let me tell you. I learned to drive off the tee with one arm, and how to chip. I could chip pretty damned good, you know. The trouble came with putting. I just couldn't get enough touch on the club to have the putts go just right. At least I can fish.

Is it easy to fish? I said.

I had to teach myself all over. But I've had a lot of practice and it's like second nature now. Want to come with me today?

Sure.

I was eleven and felt that it was about time I was let go fishing with Uncle Jake. I knew I'd get grief from mom, but that would be after I had gone. Going was what counted.

Jake had another beer then we were ready. I thought

about leaving a note for my folks saying I'd gone out on my bike but I knew they'd smell the cigarette smoke and see that two beers were gone, so I wrote on a piece of scrap paper, *Out, gone fishing*, and left it on the kitchen table. Then I went into the cellar and got my stained fishing vest, a net, and my old Mitchell spinning outfit.

Jake drove a battered Mercedes coupe convertible this summer. The thing was so noisy we had to shout to talk.

Jake said, Didn't your dad get you a fly rod?

No.

Jake nodded. He went far along the rolling hills to Stockton. We parked along the canal.

I tied on a crawfish lure. Jake took a fly rod, a five-weight, out of its case and put it together, a long, stiff brown willow switch. Then he brought out a fly reel. It was an old one, I could tell, that was well-kept and shiny, its brassy metal clean. The holes in the side of the spool reminded me of the hub-caps on new model sports cars. It was loaded with dull brown line. He secured it in the cuffs on the rod butt that was elongated like a spinning rod handle. Jake told me the butt was long so the reel was in front of his shoulder when he tucked the rod under his left arm so he was able to turn the crank with his right hand.

Jake took a leader from a leather booklet and tied it on to the line, fitting the loop ends of the line and leader with deft movements of his real fingers. He said a friend tied his leaders and flies for him. Always be grateful for that, he told me. Be grateful for a friend who'll take the time to tie knots for you. Then he took out a green Woolly Bugger from a box in his pouch and tied this on the leader. I watched how he did this. He hooked the fly into his fake index finger and fit the line through the eye of the hook, then he twirled the line with his fingers, fit the tag end through the first loop, then the second, then wetted the knot with mouth and bit the tag end with his front teeth and pulled in all directions.

I said, Do you always have to put everything together like that every time?

He smiled his crooked smile. It's part of what it is, he said. He attached a stripping basket to his belt. The breeze blew his blonde hair around and I wondered why Jake looked younger than my mother when, in fact, he was almost five years older. He seemed so young he may have been my brother.

We walked down in front of the old millhouse. The river was low and the long spit of rocks reached far out. We walked in our river sneakers until we got to the water's edge. Standing on the small, round rocks we studied the current. A fast run passed in front of us. Downwater the river turned around a narrow rocky peninsula, frothed over the rocks, and emptied into a deep eddy. I knew there was a sandbar there between the fast and slow water.

Jake said, Here's something a normal man can't do. He bent back his rubber pinky and ring fingers together at a sharp angle, then bent and kinked his middle and index fingers together into the profile of a spoon. He walked out into the water, the rod tucked under his left arm as he used a broom stick in his right hand to probe the river bottom. He went out until he was up to the ends of is shorts. He tied the leather cord on the stick through a belt loop and let the stick float behind his legs. Then he began to work the fly line.

With the bent-back pinky and ring fingers of his fake hand he culled line from the reel, his ratcheting elbow locked in place. He stripped out many feet of line that fell in the basket; he was unable to hold the coils and the current would sweep them away otherwise. Skillfully he used the rod to create a longer and longer line in the air. Then Jake stripped more line with his fingers, and with his real wrist and hand sent this line out in a sharp forward cast. I watched the Woolly Bugger ride out then dive into the water like big bee changing direction. Obviously he put it right where he wanted it. The fly and the line sank. Jake gave it a few twitches, let it drift and twitched it again, stripped line and twitched it. He let it ride the current, stripped it several times, then shot it out of the water with a quick motion of wrist and forearm and began to create another cast.

At first I wasn't sure how he was bringing line in with his fake hand, so I walked a little closer to him—I hadn't yet made a cast at all—and I watched. The brown line contrasted against his black hand and I saw how he did it.

With the line cinched in the fingers of his right hand against the cork handle, he used the spoon of his index and middle rubber fingers to pull the line, then he swung his whole arm out using his shoulder and the line jumped to the back of his fake ring and pinky fingers. This created enough tension so that he could strip a little bit. Sometimes he had to try two or three times to get the line right across his unfeeling rubber fingers, and he watched his fake hand with quick downward glances.

I nearly said, Why don't you use a push-button Zebco? but stopped myself. I stopped because he reminded me of someone. A man who spun plates on the ends of sticks? A juggler? I didn't know what he reminded me of and I didn't know what to make of his want to fish this way because it looked like a damn lot of work.

I cast with the Mitchell. I felt the little lure bounce

off rocks as it made its wiggly way in the water. Evening was upon us and I figured the fishing would pick up as the sun got low.

Jake had the first strike. A smallmouth flashed on the surface, shaking itself madly. The fish didn't take much line. Jake pinched his index and middle fingers together on the handle to hold the line, letting it slip when the fish pulled and when he stripped it with the other hand. When he had the fish in close, he called to me, I'm going to bring him near you. You net him.

Okay, I said and took up the net that hung down the back of my thigh from my belt and began walking toward him.

I was amazed at how well the fly rod worked because it was so long. That sounds obvious and elementary, but if you've never seen someone use a light, long rod to catch a fish, you don't know until you've seen so for real, up close, and I didn't know until then. As Jake held the rod up, the angle of the line gave the illusion that the fish was caught by a line tied to a tall sapling.

With a turn of his body, Jake brought the fish just in front of me. I leaned over and had the little bass in the net. I walked to the rocks where Jake met me. He said, Go ahead and unhook him. If I were alone I'd do it myself with pliers. I'm not too proud to ask. He laughed at himself. I had the fish by the lower lip and pulled the hook out carefully, then I handed Jake the fly. He looked it over in the palm of its hand, then he said, Hold him up.

I held the bass up and turned it so the sun shone on the length of its body. It was maybe one pound. Its body shone like a million tiny tiles of dark amber. I dipped the fish back in the river and moved it back and forth for a moment, then it disappeared with a slight jolt to my fingers.

Very fine for so little work, Jake said and walked back out into the water using the broomstick. He lobbed the Woolly Bugger in the air to dry it. I made a long cast and began working the crawfish again, boggling my mind for what it was Jake reminded me of. A fencer? I had a very good strike and fought something that pulled and turned again and again, then flopped out of the water once, a stout smallmouth. It turned and turned again with the current until I fought it into the shallows at my left near some exposed rocks. It jumped once again, a catapulting jump, and the lure shot out of its mouth like a slow bullet. The fish hung there a moment, long enough for both Jake and I to see how lovely it was, its body burning like tiger's eye. When it hit the water it was gone forever.

I didn't curse though I could have. I shook my head, embarrassed to look at Uncle Jake. He said, Don't tell me that wasn't a beautiful thing.

I won't, I said.

By then the sun was mottled by small, hazy clouds as it turned red and slid down. The sky took on a bluish cast over head. The air was warm. I wondered if my mother had ever seen Jake fish; I wondered if it would matter to her that he obviously had some kind of talent he enjoyed. I wondered what she wanted from him, or what she wanted him to do. He seemed such a capable man to me that I found it hard not to like him, and hard not to think my mother was a bit vindictive. Some people just don't turn out perfect like you and dad, I said to her as I fished.

In the beautiful gloom of summer sundown, as Jake came to look at a fat smallmouth I had netted for him, I saw a look in his eyes. It was a relaxed gaze, his eyes focused as they always were, but open, absorbing. His shirt was stained dark under is arms, and his brow was beaded with sweat. He seemed to like being hot and used up because of all his motion to make one cast, swim the streamer along, and cast it again. Once when he had a bass that made a wide run to the right, he cursed because the fish ran into the current, then doubled back on the slack line, and Jake had to quickly haul the slack with his black fingers. The turn this fish made was a very good strategy, he remarked to me later— Almost as if he knew I had a bad arm, Jake said. He landed the fish a little way up the bank. It was a nice one, maybe two pounds, that he steered on the taut leader and pulled into a few inches of water. He tucked the rod under his left arm, put line in his mouth, clamping it with his lips, and shoved his thumb in the fish's mouth. He held it up for me to see.

I'm guessing that's how he did it. I wasn't able to see all that from where I stood but after thinking about it since that day, that's how he must have done it. I'm sure I did see him put the line in his mouth.

The sun went down behind the hills. I put my Mitchell down on the rocks and watched Jake. My shoulders twitched as I imaged how I could use the fly rod. I watched Jake's right arm move with his casts. His arm moved smoothly, so smooth it seemed to go too slowly. His head jutted a little like a rooster's as he brought the line forward. He looked exactly where he wanted the fly to go; he never looked back at his line. With my sixth grade learning I was pleased to think that he formed an isosceles triangle: his line of vision one triangle leg, his arm the base, the finished cast the other leg.

I waded out next to him on his left. The water came up past my waist. I said, Can I try?

He said, Yeah, why don't you.

He stripped in most of the line and wound it into the reel. He walked around behind me, put the rod in my right hand, and walked off to my left. He coached me through a few awkward slashes of the rod, then I got out about fifteen feet of line and got it to move nicely in the air. It reminded me of an old cane pole I once had.

Jake said, Don't take it out to the side so far. More straight up and down. Look back at the line. Elbow in tight.

I looked back at the dark line against the rocks and trees. I brought it back around too soon and made a whipping sound. I didn't get frustrated, and Jake was a smart coach. After a while I had learned to get the line to finish just right on my back cast and bring it forward without any harsh snapping sound. I wondered if I could learn to do anything.

Jake asked if he may get in a few more casts and he took the rod back. I made a few casts again with the plug. We caught nothing. We quit when the sky was a blue-brown and Jake was unable to see exactly where the Woolly Bugger hit; we saw the line, but we didn't see the dive of the fly, so that was how we told time. We walked back to the car and sat on the hood. I took the crawfish off my line and dried it. I had caught four smallmouth, the biggest a pound and a half maybe, but it had flown through the air so nicely it didn't matter if it weighed no more than a paper fish.

I wanted to ask Jake how he began to fly fish, and why he liked it so much because I was still wondering what I thought about when I watched him. Instead I said, Jake, what happened to your arm?

My real arm, you mean?

Yeah.

I figured she wouldn't have told you.

No. She doesn't mention you much.

Jake laughed a little, without sound, just so his body shrugged. He looked back out to the river. The river was a shiny slick in the dark. Jake had taken five fish and was clearly very pleased. He was sweaty and smelled like tree sap from the folds of his shirt. He said, This was one of the best evenings of fishing I've ever had. I put on one Woolly Bugger, never switched it, and I made every cast just like I hoped, and fought every fish just like I hoped, and they were just right. Didn't lose the Bugger, didn't break the leader. You see these guys on Tv who go out there with all that gear and all that horsepower to catch fish so big—he leaned back, threw out his arms wide, and sighed. He lit a cigarette from the pack in his shirt pocket, the long rod across his knees. He blew smoke and it rose against the black trees and disappeared in the dark sky.

He said, Your mother was the one who blew off my arm.

I sucked in my breath.

He nodded, pulling on the cigarette. He said, You can't ever tell her I told you. She doesn't want you to know this, and one of the smartest things you'll ever learn is how to pretend you don't know things.

What happened? I said.

He snickered. He said, It was really stupid, actually. It was my fault.

He continued, When we were kids, we used to play robbers. Not cops and robbers, just robbers. The object of the game was to ambush the other person, anywhere, anyhow, and rob them. We had all sorts of cap guns and water pistols. One day I was was giving your mother shit about being a girl and not knowing how to use a real gun. I said this, I think, because she'd tried to twirl a six-shooter with both hands. Well, she was ambidextrous. She could use both hands, but when she put them both out with a cap gun in each hand, she pointed them funny, like pigeon toes because her hands couldn't coordinate together completely like that. I understand that perfectly now because of this goddamned thing. He waved his black arm from the shoulder.

He said, She must have pointed a couple of six shooters at me one day and I think I said something like, "Girly girl can't point 'em straight." You know how older brothers act. They make a little sister want to intimidate them back.

I agreed, nodding. I had a sister three years younger than I was and a rap sheet of meanness.

Jake put the glinting reel in its pouch after he thought the line had dried enough. Then he carefully took the rod apart and put it in its case. He stubbed his cigarette on the gravel. He said, I was down in the cellar working on a balsa wood airplane, a biplane, I remember. I heard something behind me. I turned and there was Peggie, your mother, and she had this big damned shotgun slung up at me. She said, "It's robbers, boy," and began pulling on the trigger. That trigger had about a six-pound pull and she was really yanking on it. I threw up my arms. I was trying to wave at her, not stick my hands up like I was playing the game, like it was a stick up. All I remember is that I just got my hands up and there was a wide flash all over me. Then I was in the driveway. Dad was standing over me. Then I was in an ambulance. Then I was in the hospital.

When I woke up in the hospital, my arm hurt so bad. Jake gestured with the false arm. I mean, it felt like it was in a vice, from the elbow down. I was really groggy and messed up from the anesthetic and I kept telling everyone that my arm hurt. I was trying to look down at it, and I remember once I did look down and I couldn't see it, so I thought I was sleeping on it tucked behind me and that was why it hurt so much. But every time I tried to see where it was dad pushed me back down and told me to rest.

Darkness filled in around us.

He said, For a long time she didn't talk to me. Not at all. I was really angry. I had wanted to play football, but now there was no way. I couldn't fish properly. I had a hard time trying to get girls to dance with me at school dances. Some would dance with me because they liked me, but I could see how funny they felt. I watched their faces and they had an extra big smile like they were saying, "No, Jake, it doesn't bother me that you've only got one arm. I didn't ever notice."

He laughed. He said, I don't know why I let it get to me. They were just high school girls. Don't ever marry a high school girl. I got married while I was in college, and I dropped out of college. I married the only girl who seemed like she really liked me when we were in high school. You know what she is now?

I shrugged.

You know what? he said, insisting.

What?

She's a nun, he shouted. A nun. A nun! Can you believe that? and he laughed aloud. It was the easiest divorce of my life, he said. And we still write to each other. Her name was Jill. She was really nice. Too pretty to be a nun.

Jake lit a cigarette and blew smoke. We listened to the distant sound of the river washing over the rocks. I pictured the swirl of fly line in the air. He said, Let's go. I'll explain it all to your folks why you're out past dark.

I realized we had been gone for a long time and I was bordering on being grounded because the note I had left—"Out, gone fishing"—was not very specific.

As we rode in the car, Jake shouted over the engine

and slipstream. Your mother and I didn't talk for a long time. She once came up to my room and said she was sorry, then she got upset and ran away while I was trying to tell her I forgave her. I did, but I was still pretty angry. You just don't get an arm blown off without getting really angry. Peggie knew I was angry. I think she's been tougher on herself about this than I ever would have. So, since that day, a lot went by between us. Everything changed. We sure as hell didn't play robbers anymore. We really didn't do much together anymore. That was pretty bad. I wish I did something about that then.

How did you get this arm? I said.

This is a pretty nice thing, isn't it? A buddy of mine is a machinist. He makes prosthetics for Vietnam Vets. He used to make bicycle parts and exercise machine parts, but then he began to make custom limbs. I got together a bunch of money and went to Atlantic city and played craps. It wasn't easy. I had to go back a few times, but I made about double what I had, so I paid him to make it. It's a damned nice improvement over what I had when I was younger. You should have seen the crappy things they gave me. Shit, I would have been as well off with a stick I picked up in the yard. The first arm I had was this piece of glossy flesh-colored plastic like something for a G.I. Joe doll with a steel hook on the end. Try to pick your nose with that.

You were left-handed?

Yeah, I was. Now I'm not either. It's like I've got one strong arm and one strong hand right in the middle of my chest.

She just blew your arm clean off?

Not clean off, but it was so ragged they couldn't reattach it.

I wanted to ask him what happened right after he was

shot but I couldn't.

Jake pulled into the driveway. He said, I'll tell them I gave you a fly fishing lesson and we lost track of time. They'll blame me. Easy.

We got out of the convertible and went inside. My parents and sister were watching Tv. For one of those few, unknown magical reasons, mom and dad weren't angry at all. They seemed whimsical. They were even happy to see Jake. We all went out on the patio, lit citronella candles and talked. My father and Jake had some Scotch, and so did my mother, and my sister and I ate sherbet.

The rest of that night Jake talked about fishing. He said he planned to go up to Canada to go fly fishing for salmon the next year, and I wanted to say, Take me with you, but I knew he was just talking. He was trying to make my mother like him; trying to make her believe he didn't care anymore, and make her believe that he was able and had a good life. But I realized that even if I told her that Jake had taught himself to fly fish with that black arm she would still feel the same. Neither of them were able to let go the difference between themselves.

I thought of what it was Jake made me think of while I had watched him cast. I didn't figure it out then. I've only just figured it out. He was a painter who was allowed a finite number of gestures placed exactly in the right spots, in the right way, to make a canvas bisected by perfectly placed dots that painted a river.

FOUR

Golfing Buddies

This is a story about my friend John, who I like and admire. I like and admire him especially for what he did to golf.

John is very crafty. He is crafty mostly about his fly fishing.

John is also crafty about his name and appearance. His full name is John Irving, just like the novelist. And perhaps due to a kind of collective genetics, he almost looks exactly like John Irving, the novelist: strongly built, full, handsome Irish face, heavy eyebrows, intense dark eyes, and longish iron-grey hair. Once, he and his girlfriend, and I and my wife, stayed at a hotel in Vermont for a fishing vacation. One morning in the lobby a nice elderly woman saw him, went up to him, and said, Are you...*John Irving*? John smiled slyly and said, Yes, m'am. She told him how much she liked his novels. He thanked her graciously and asked her to be sure to buy the next one.

This past fall, I went over to John's house to watch a football game. He and Kelly, his girlfriend, were sitting in the living room drinking beers and jeering the Eagles. I noticed a stack of books on the dining table. I asked him what they were. He said, I bumped into this guy at the library last week. He asked me if I was John Irving and I said I was. He got all excited and asked me if he could send me some books to sign.

I went over and looked at the books. They were novels, John Irving's novels, *the* John Irving, all of them first editions: *Setting Free the Bears*, *The Cider House Rules*, *Hotel New Hampshire*, *The 158-Pound Marriage*, *A Prayer for Owen Meany*, *The Water Method Man*, *The World According to Garp*, and *Son of the Circus*. I looked over at John. He smiled. John, I said, you're not going to sign these.

He shrugged. Kelly looked at him, shook her head, and turned back to the Tv. I said, John, these are first editions. You'll ruin them if you sign them. They're be considered forgeries and have no value.

John said, I'll sign them in the back on the fly leaf.

I shook my head, grabbed a beer, and sat down to watch the game. A week later when I came by to borrow a saw, I noticed that the books were gone. Some poor, excited academic was somewhere cooing over his collection of signed John Irving first editions.

But this story isn't about books. It's about fly fishing, and golf.

I don't play golf much. I've played a few times in the past couple years and done poorly but had fun. My father was a good golfer but he seemed put upon to have to get up early for a tee time. I realized later he golfed for business purposes, because when he retired he started playing tennis.

Many people, I think, put golf and fly fishing close by in sports categories because fly fishing and golf are both outdoor sports pursued in the countryside. They also are not contact sports, do not require pads, and do not require the participant to be in tip-top shape or very young. They also have a high pricetag, although golf is consistently pricey; fly fishing is costly when you must travel or get a new rod, which isn't all the time.

John Irving loved one and despised the other, for deep personal reasons. When he had the chance to strike a deadly blow to the spongy rubber heart of golf, he took it.

John Irving, the novelist, was once a wrestler. My John Irving played football, in high school and in college. He nearly turned pro, but broke his ankle his last season. After the knee, the ankle is the next most important joint. So he became a phys-ed instructor at a prep school nearby where he and I live now. He started playing football, though, to get revenge on his own father.

John's father was a successful engineer, and was also a semi-pro golfer for a while. Very early in John's life his father, Vincent Irving, put a golf club in his hands and coached him relentlessly. Sometimes this produces a Tiger Woods. Other times it produces an angry son.

John and I met when we were both thirteen years old because our fathers played at the same country club outside Villanova and entered themselves in father-son golf tournaments. The first time I saw John he and his father were in one of those intense father-to-son arguments engaged with taut jaws, hoarse, spittle-shot whispers, and red faces. Whatever they fought over, his father won, and John went to his bag, pulled out an iron, and let fly a decent shot to the green.

All along, John built his case against the game, stroke by stroke. It just wasn't that he hated to be forced to do something the right way—he hated the thing itself. He said to me later that golf is mere physics, and if you like that, then shoot pool and be done with it.

The moment John had the chance to join the football team at our high school he did so to irk his father, who thought contact sports were for meat heads. John was big, and he was fast. He played both offense and defense, and he had so many girlfriends he made the rest of us look bad.

Yet when we talked on the phone after his ankle was plastered and his shot at the pros was gone, he told me, I shouldn't have played it anyway. I wasn't true to it.

Soon after that he started fly fishing seriously, not just chucking a line around when there was no wind. He and his father by then were not speaking and he communicated to his parents through his two sisters. His mother, who loved John's first wife, found out about his first then second divorces weeks after they occurred.

This whole diabolical story begins at a Christmas party at a big house in one of the big developments surrounding my little town like slow panzer divisions. I forget how or why both John and I and our respective mates were there; friend of a friend, I guess. I was pulled into a discussion about golf.

I spoke with these two fellows who I had met before—Colin, and Brent. I don't remember where I'd met them. They looked like male models from the L.L. Bean catalog: mid-30s, not thin but trim, married to good-looking L.L. Beanesque wives. I had to get past these men to get to the punch bowl, and when we noticed each other, I said, Hey, I know you. You guys golf.

Soon we were embroiled in a discussion of preseason course maintenance, which told me these guys were nuts. They asked me if I golfed. I said that I did not. Colin asked, Then what do you do?

I fly fish.

He said, Isn't that the kind of fishing where you flick

it out there again and again so it looks like a fly flying around?

I smiled and said, Yeah, kind of like that. I saw John nearby. The thought of him squaring off with these two was an idea too entertaining to pass up. I called him over. I introduced him to Colin and Brent then told him they were interested in fly fishing.

Yeah, Colin said. I've always wanted to give it a try.

John said, Have you ever tried at all?

Both men said no. John asked what they played. They said simultaneously, Golf.

Oh, John said, dipping the ladle in the punch bowl with a bow.

But how does the fish get to the fly? Brent asked. They leap from the water at it?

John's said cordially, No, not like that. You get the imitation fly to land on the water. It sits there. The trout sees it, swims up, and eats it.

The two golfers nodded, saying, Oh.

Colin said, Um, how do you get into it? What sort of equipment do you need?

Are you guys serious golfers? John said.

Yes, said one.

Very, said the other.

John gulped his punch. He said, Fly fishing is like golf. It takes a lot of time and effort. It might take away from your golf game.

Why would it? Colin asked.

You have to be dedicated to it, I said, keeping my hand in. Looking back I see that John and I quietly threw down the gauntlet. But what he said next surprised me.

Well, John said, if you're keen on it, you two should take it up.

Really? Brent said. He was larger and blonder than

Colin and could have played football with John.

Sure, John said. It does give you something you can relax with. After a hard day of golf, you could spend a lovely evening on the river casting for bass.

I almost said something to John, but his sincerity stopped me. He never acted like this, especially with two blockheads like these. Was he trying to make new friends? Soon the two golfers and the fisherman were talking seriously about getting together to go fly fishing. They exchanged phone numbers. Brent asked John if he had e-mail and John shook his head. You've got to get e-mail, Brent said. John nodded, smiling, then he and I downed our punch and ladled out more to ourselves as the golfers moved away.

John, I said, I hope you plan something awful for those two.

He looked askance at me. And there you were telling me not to sign first editions of novels with my own name, he said.

That's different, I said. That's forgery and deceit.

But I am John Irving.

Why were you playing nice with those two?

Because they were getting that look in their eye, the look that all golfers get when talking about another sport—a look that says, "Not as good as golf." I beat them to the punch. If they're serious, then what I'll do is make fly fishing seem so awful and stupid they'll never take it up. And you know what?

What?

If just one guy like me would do that for every two yahoos who have no reason to take up fly fishing, the sport would eventually be cleansed of all idiots who don't need to be on the water.

True, I said.

You know the Scots invented golf, don't you?

Yes, I said.

Wrong. Some yahoo in Florida combined pin-ball and croquet and got golf. Back in the nineteen-twenties.

Seriously?

Seriously.

I didn't see John through the rest of that winter, though I spoke with him over the telephone several times. I was very ill with flu on the Super Bowl weekend when John has a big party, and ill for several weeks more and not up for a night at the pub. Then for my wife's birthday, she and I got a cheap flight to Florida and went there for a week. The sun burned off my sickness and I came home well.

April brings the early hatches. I went to Creighty's sporting goods store in Newtown one day to buy some leader when I saw something that made me stop in my tracks: John Irving was standing at the glass-topped counter with Brent and Colin, a fly reel in his hand. He was talking to them, and Creighty, the old guy who ran the store, was looking at John with delighted eyes. Obviously John was telling to two golfers what fly reel to buy. The two men who were used to spending upwards of $200 on a single golf club figured that they could spare the same amount for a reel that would last them a lifetime. John later told me that Brent and Colin spent a combined total of $1,600 in Creighty's store that day.

Lefty Kreh never had disposable income like that when he started, I'm sure.

In the very early part of the season I went to the river to try for shad on the fly and caught a few scrappy bucks. I waited for the weather to heat up a little. On the right days, I went to the Little Lehigh and drove out to beleaguered Spring Creek, catching ten fish during the second week of May on Blue Quills and Griffith's Gnats. I called John then. I said, Have you been out to the Juniata yet?

Yeah. I did all right, he said.

I heard voices in the background. I said, You've got company?

Just Brent and Colin.

What?

I'm telling them about smallmouth.

Why in the hell are you doing that?

They asked, he said. They want to go fishing on the river.

John, I said, do you think giving them so much help is a good idea?

I thought you were with me on this.

I'm not sure what I'm with.

You started it back at the Christmas party.

What have I started?

John said, Come on over and help, all right?

Help what? I said.

Brent and Colin are interested in smallmouth. You've fished for smallmouth all your life. We need your expertise.

I hung up, put on a jacket, and told Pat, my wife, that I was going over to John's. She looked up from her book and said, Are you going to be long?

I don't know, I said.

What are you and John up to? she said. She liked John, but trusted him not at all, and did not trust me with him.

I don't know, I said again. He's got some friends he wants to teach about fly fishing.

I walked over the soggy, mowed field then through

the trees to get to John's house. Spring was full in the air, but the nights were still a bit cold. My Florida tan had faded. I went down the lane, up on John's porch, and turned the knob to ring the bell. Kelly opened the door and smiled at me, aware that her man and I were up to no good. She said, What is he doing with these two preppies?

He's teaching them to fly fish.

She shook her head, the finger of one hand drawn across her mouth. Len, she said, he's up to no good. I know it. She studied me with her big, clear green eyes.

I shrugged. I walked into the low-ceilinged, wood-hued den, and was faced with a Clouser's Minnow held in the air. Colin, pasty-faced of winter, lurched into me and said, Do you think that looks like a minnow?

I stopped, drew my breath, and saw John in a chair in the corner. He glanced at me with a flicker of his eyes. I turned back to the streamer before me. I said, I think a Clouser's Minnow is like a shaving foam brush. But bass like them, so I say they look tasty.

Colin pulled the streamer back to his breast and studied it in his hand. He said, But why does it look edible to a smallmouth bass?

Are you trying to define what looks tasty to a fish? I said.

There's got to be some reason behind it, he said, nearly indignant. Why would a fish eat it otherwise?

I glanced at John, then at Brent, who stood by the long desk that John used for reading, writing, and tying flies. Brent looked at me keenly, as if I held the secret to Clouser's Minnows and other streamers. I looked back to Colin. He was looking at me too. I said, Colin, there are certain things that you have to go on faith with. That's the religion of the sport. Have you ever seen old-style salmon flies?

No.

They're colored like butterflies.

Only dry flies make sense to me, Colin said.

Why? I said.

Because they look like flies. They look real. But this thing—he held up the minnow—this looks like a short paintbrush.

I told them that streamers look much different when swimming in the current. A general discussion ensued about what a fly was supposed to look like; both Colin and Brent seemed at a loss of imagination to make the leap from Hendricksons and Comparaduns to Mickey Finns, and Deceivers. Ultimately, to my chagrin, they were intensely intrigued rather than put off.

After they left, each saying they had to help their wives with dinner, I sat down with a brandy next to John. I said, Jesus Christ, they're gung-ho.

John smiled. Yes, he said, they are just what I want. They are literalists. That comes from playing golf. Golf is all tangibles and tangents, strokes and vectors. It's geometry and physics. There's no imagination. No fakery. No *art*. You can play bold and force your way over the course, but it's still very logical.

So? I said. Tying flies and fishing them right seems pretty logical to me.

But that's how I'm going to get them. I'm going to infuse their brains with the worry over looks and movement. What worse things could throw off a golfer than worrying how his stroke *appears* or how he reacts to different lighting conditions?

You can't be serious, I said. These guys have got handicaps down to scratch. You think that concerns of one sport can corrupt their expertise at another?

Just enough grit in the engine, John said.

I took a big sip of brandy. I said, Is this about your

father?

No, he said, not indignant but sure. Dad has nothing to do with this.

I frowned.

Okay, he said, maybe this is all about that, those days. But these two golfers think fly fishing is going to be a lark. They think it's going to be a recreation to take their minds off golf. How many of these self-satisfied dorks are out there screwing around rod in hand right now?

I don't think they could really harm fly fishing, John. Atheists and snake handlers haven't smashed the Anglican Church.

Why shouldn't I prove to a couple of them that their sport is not superior? John said.

I'm with you on that, I said. I just don't see the method.

John lurched forward in the chair. He said, I'm going to make it easy on them at first. I'm going to take them out on the river and hook them up to a couple small-mouth, maybe even a good striper or two. Then I'm going to let them go on their own. They'll screw up at some point and go back to golf. They'll always carry that doubt with them that they screwed up at a sport. And they won't be able to figure out why. Well, that *why* is that fishing is a real sport and golf isn't.

I frowned at him again.

John insisted, Golf is a fiction. It's about landscaping and how well the grass is mowed. It's got nothing on fishing of any kind. We go after animals that are craftier than us. Aren't they?

I finished the brandy. I said, Yes. Why do you want to prove that?

Sitting back in the chair he said, Well, to entertain myself and to prove myself right.

I didn't laugh but I smiled. John, you're a son of a bitch, I said.

Will you help me?

How?

Just be my witness when I need you.

This is about a lot of stuff you hated growing up, right?

It's about everything, he said.

I said, Keep me posted. Then I went home. Pat smirked at the story I told her, but what I told her was a careful lie that she did not even sense when we went to bed. I told her that John was trying to impress someone enough to get access to fish on private land.

A few weeks later he called. He said he had taken Colin and Brent out on the Delaware and had caught numerous smallmouth, one going 15 inches, and several nice spring-run stripers chasing the first waves of herring. Colin and Brent had golfed all morning and early afternoon, gone home, changed, and they and John fished until after sundown.

John said, It was just like a cross between a beer commercial and the J. Crew catalog. They even took me out for drinks afterward. They want to go again next weekend.

How was their casting? I said.

Passable. They got the streamer out there, but I had to remind them now and then about certain things.

Can they tie knots?

Actually, they can.

Do they know when to change flies? I said.

I told them what to put on and when to switch, but next time I won't.

John, I said, aren't you afraid this thing is going to backfire?

Give it time. Right now they're having their honeymoon. Eventually they're going to have a few bad days. That's when the vibes will start.

What vibes?

John said, The vibes in their head. *I can't master fly fishing. How can that be? I'm so good at golf.* Pretty soon after that the vibe will be there all the time. Bango— handicap goes up a stroke. Then they're really freaked out.

This is wishful thinking, I said.

It's masterful thinking, John said, with the aplomb that allows him to impersonate a famous writer. I need you to come along next time, Len, he said. I need a pro like you who doesn't want to play nice with them. I really want you to show them how it's done. That will get their blood up.

So, a week later I was out there around the islands above Scudder's Falls, which aren't really falls but a series of shallow rapids with a deep, frothing sluice over on the Jersey side where kyakers practice. The Delaware was slightly up but was clear and wadeable.

The act of wading, however, is always dicey. Colin slipped, fell, and went under. At the time I had a very good smallmouth on but began to walk toward the fallen man who was bouncing along just under the surface, his 6-weight sticking up like a feeble antenna. John got to him just as Colin found his footing and tried to stand. He cursed several times very loudly, then marched to the bank to take off his waders. John was friend and brother to the wet golfer. Brent laughed and snorted and Colin yelled at him. When I pulled out my third smallmouth over 12 inches they all shut up. John smiled at me. I was doing my job. I was making it look easy, but what helped greatly was a change in the weather. This night was cool and cloudy after two days of warm. The smallmouth were hunting and were hitting anything white. When my white Woolly Bugger broke off on a rock, I tied on a Schenk's White Streamer and did just as well. Colin and Brent were using olive Woolly Buggers, and John fished a black one to seem just as luckless. They caught a few small smallmouth, which is all right, really, but they saw me, searched their boxes and found nothing white. John took the opportunity to point out that a good fly box always has all kinds of colors of different flies, and then a few kickers too boot, like a big stonefly imitation or a water pup just in case. The two men seemed to study John's words, then returned to casting, glancing at me when John told them to watch how well I cast. That was when Colin fell.

I walked over to the soaked man. He was wringing out his socks. I said, Just wade in your jeans now, cause it's gonna feel awful when you put the waders back on.

Yeah, but my sneakers are back in the car, he said.

I offered him one of my white streamers. Take it, I told him. You need a change of luck.

This, of course, was almost a way of cursing someone, to talk about his luck to his face then offer him a fly, but he took the streamer from me. I then gave my other to Brent, who also accepted, thanking me sincerely. I went over to John. How'm I doing?

He smiled and nodded. He was tying on a bright yellow Marabou Mickey. He looked at me. He said, Kelly is on to what I'm doing.

You've got to keep this one, John. She's the only one who's learned you through and through and still likes you.

Yeah, but I'd better not marry her. I always loose them when I do that.

No, don't marry her, I said. Just make her understand it is very much worth her while to stay. Don't cheat.

You know I don't cheat.

But that's how your first marriage ended.

I didn't cheat, Len, I fell in love. Husbands who cheat run around all the time screwing anything. I met someone else and realized I had married the wrong person.

That's cheating of the highest order, I told him.

Brent began yelling. We looked. His rod was bent. His drag even buzzed. But then the fish was off. He said, Damn, like a surprised kid.

John muttered, That was good. He lost a big fish. Probably a nice striper.

Colin braved the cold water, cursed, put his waders back on, and just before full darkness he called it quits. This, I'm sure John thought, was a very good outcome: one somewhat happy golfer, and one wet, very unhappy golfer. This could create discord in their golfing partnership and cause them trouble in the upcoming invitational tournament at their country club.

We decamped to John's house for beers. Before the night was through, John said to the two golfers, Now, listen, guys, I've done nearly enough already. The time has come for you to go fishing on your own. I usually fish alone or with Len. Sometimes you can drag me out, but you're only going to learn by doing.

Brent and Colin nodded. When they left the house, they said they'd stay in touch through the summer.

Think they'll make it? I said.

All they've got are a box each of streamers I tied, a few leaders, one reel and one rod apiece, he said. I've hardly told them anything about dries.They won't get the hang of it and it will bother them, and they're not the type to go to instructional classes.

He spoke with surety. I studied his face, his black eye brows hunched together over his intense eyes. I said,

This whole wager depends on the implicit assumption you've made that a person cannot love and excel at two sports.

He nodded. No one can. Doesn't work that way. Not in one's heart. There's just that one sport you love the most. They love golf.

Yes, they do, I said.

How can you love a physical endeavor that's so abstract?

I like pool, I said.

John shook his head. Golf is wrong, he said.

Kelly came in and said to us, The two of your are evil.

Through June and into July I fished a lot, using mostly Drakes and Sulphurs. Pat and I took a trip to the upper Delaware. Pat doesn't fish, but she likes the scenery. Sometimes she sits in a two-man inflatable raft anchored in the water so we can talk while I fish. She brings her books. She works as a librarian at a nearby college library, and loves books as objects as much as she likes them as literature. If I had told her about John's forgeries she would have gone over to his house and punched him in the nose.

While glancing at my wife as she lay in the raft near-by, I started to doubt John. What he was doing was wholly unsportsmanlike. What was worse than my commiseration with John in his plot was the delight I drew from it. For some reason I wanted to see both Brent and Colin fail miserably. I am also sure that John's interest did not wholly rise out of his hatred of golf, though he does truly, purely hate it; nor was his meanness completely rooted in his long-ago contest with his father. He wanted to see two men fail because he made them fail, and this, I could only decide, grew out of some true malice, possibly an evil, that inhabited his soul. All this talk about assaulting golf itself was propaganda.

As I cast into the amber wash the sun made of the river, I shook my head, doubting myself. I caught three fat rainbow trout and let them go.

John, I said into the telephone, why don't we just stop this right now? It's stupid.

Come on, Len. Have some fun.

Why do this?

You started it.

I did not start it, I said. All I did was introduce the three of you.

But you knew they were golfers and you called me over to make fun of them at that party.

What if I did?

Now I'm making fun of them.

Then if I started it I want it to stop, I said. So stop, please, John.

I can't, he said. I'm having fun.

I sighed. I didn't know what to say. I finally said, Give me one good reason why you are abusing these two men.

It's like I said. They think they're masters. Not all golfers are like that, but some are. They think that if you master golf all else is child's play. I want to disabuse them of that. And in that way we're not abusing them, we're abusing golf. We're attacking an abstract, you know, like trying to blow-up Greenwich Mean Time with a bomb. We're attacking landscaping and grounds keeping. We're attacking snooty country clubs and golf carts. We're attacking poly-cotton blend trousers!

Not to mention all the herbicide and pesticide, I said.

Yes! John boomed. They want me to go fishing with them again. Now that they've got the bug, we'll get them the cure.

Sure we will.

Come with me, John said.

Where?

Way up at Stockton. We'll fish that whole section.

Why not? I said.

A few days later we were up there. John and I did all right but our two Arnie Palmers were pulling them in, not big ones, but in numbers—a schoolie, then a small-mouth, then another smallmouth. Brent eventually netted a 20-inch striper, quite a catch in the current.

In the gathering dark I said to John, Let's get them out of here now.

Why? They might fall in the dark. Be a good lesson.

Because, I said, they just might notice the bass feeding on caddisflies and really get some ideas. Listen.

Around us were *plunks* and *ploogs* of smallmouth eating flies off the surface. I had seen this happen dozens of times before and not been able to catch a fish myself which irked me to no end. I did not want these amateurs to do anything daring that paid off, in case they had been buying flies on their own. John agreed and we called Brent and Colin off the blue water and walked back to our cars. They jabbered like boy scouts after a jamboree.

Through mid-summer, Colin and Brent golfed in the mornings and fished through the evenings on the river. This is what John told me. Sometimes they called him, sometimes they went themselves. The whole plot seemed to have turned into a positive success.

John and I were sitting on his back porch in the dark after a day on the Little Lehigh, drinking lemonade. John swallowed with a loud trickle. He said, They told me they were looking in some book about hatches and said they want to try dry flies. Here is where they shall fail.

How?

I'm going to take them out some morning and make them cast Tricos. They'll never get the hang of that. I can't wait to see the look on their faces when I show them what a Trico is. Why don't you come with us?

What day?

Sunday. I convinced them to skip church. Can you believe that these guys go to church? Who goes to church anymore?

Okay, I said, I'm in.

John looked at me. He said, You've been in from the start.

Six a.m. This did not seem too awful to Brent and Colin who were used to early tee-times. John flew along the interstate in his old green Cougar. Brent and Colin followed in their Jeep Cherokee.

We parked near the railroad tunnel and broke out our gear. John handed Brent a fly box. Brent opened it and stared at the tiny black puffs of material and hook. Jeez, these are small, he said. Are these gnats?

They're Tricos. *Tricorythodes*, John said.

Colin peered into the fly box. He said, Well, now, these make sense. They look like something, like a little fly. Will big trout eat them?

If there's a hatch on, yes, I said. I shivered and sniffed. Something in the air told me this might be a very good day. West Valley Creek is a fine water. We put our hip-boots on and made our way down a trail to the stream. I whispered to John, You get the feeling they're getting good at this?

They cannot do well here, he said quietly. He was wrong.

The sun soon penetrated the darkness of the foliage. Each of us staked out a section of water and waited almost an hour as mosquitos bumped into us. I listened to the swish of the trees. As the sun lit the leaves, the Tricos appeared. I saw them almost immediately: tiny dark motes, their wings nimbused against the lightening water. An entomologist looks for insects more intently than the fly fisher, but does not seek such salvation as we do.

In front of me was a perfect riffle, ripply current curving below against a smooth swath of slack water along the weedy edge, maybe ten feet from where I crouched. I cast and the fly landed inches away from the current. Nothing hit. I cast a dozen more times, and, instead of moving, I waited and tied on a larger fly, size 22. The hatch thickened. I cast again when I saw the dimples the trout made on the surface. On the third cast I had a fish.

Moving upstream, then back, and passing few other anglers, I managed to take two brown trout in an hour. The hatch was slowing down. I went to find John. He stood near a bend where the water ran past a deep edge. I tipped my hat to him. He shook his head. Len, damn it, they're getting the hang of it, he said.

Are they?

I've mostly been watching them. They realized they had to put on bigger flies. They learned to make good roll casts. They're getting the drift right. Mending the line. I didn't tell them any of that stuff. They must be reading books.

Are they catching fish? I asked.

Yes. Three each. It's disgusting.

Just then Brent came trotting up with his net. Look, guys, he said, and held up the net. A fat, shiny brown trout was slung in the netting. It flexed its fins and snapped its jaws once. I nodded. Nice, I said. Very nice.

I've gotta keep this one. I mean, I've never caught trout until today.

Never caught trout until today—I winced; the son of a bitch has got to catch a trout like that on this stream on his first day. We told him he had to put the fish back.

Why? he said.

This is all delayed harvest, I said. Besides, it's bad luck to keep a fish the first time you catch its kind.

But I want to show it to my wife. I told her I'd bring fish back.

To eat? John said.

I think I could put this one on my wall, Brent said, but I know it's big enough to eat. Doesn't delayed harvest mean you have to put some of the fish back, not all of them?

Put it back, John said. Regulations.

Brent's expression soured then went blank. All right, he said, and walked away.

John and I watched him. He looked at the fish one more time then dipped it in the water. We saw it finning on the surface, then it turned into a thin streak of light and was gone.

By nine o'clock when the hatch was over, Brent and Colin had ten fish between them. I caught three. John caught two. Not that numbers matter, but our sense of superiority was beaten soundly by these two men new to the sport. As we drove home, John and I began to discuss the possibility that despite their chummy demeanor, lovely clothes, and good looks, Colin and

Brent were true to the sport.

Beginners luck? John said.

I don't know, I said. They blundered into it, but they had a strong sense of what they were doing.

John nodded. He said, Think we need a make-over?

A what?

A make-over. Totally new clothes and hats and stuff.

I looked at our army-surplus clothes, and the waterproof satchel that I prefer over a fishing vest. I took off my boonie hat and looked at it. It was gunked with dust, sweat, mud, and pitch. Maybe we did need a make-over.

Back at the house, Colin and Brent used John's bathroom then dashed off because they had a noon tee-time. Their smiles betrayed what they did not say. As their big Jeep disappeared, John squared his shoulders, jerked his head, and spouted at them—Fly fishing was the sport of lords long before some explorer discovered Scottish heathens running drunken and naked through a moor chasing a feather ball with their sheep hooks.

They can't hear you, John.

Golf hears me.

A few days later, Colin called John. He said, John, I'd like for you and Len to be guests at the Summer Invitational at the club.

To golf?

Ah, no, just as guests. There's a golf tournament all day for club members and association people, and then a banquet for members and guests that night. It's a really fun day. Bring your girlfriend too. And Len can bring his wife.

John was about to decline when something writhed in his heart. He said, What day?

Next Saturday. Sorry it's short notice.

John said, Well, why not?

Great, Brent said. Great.

John called me. I said, Forget it, I'm not going.

Come drink up their wine.

No thanks. Golf I don't have any grudge against. A country club banquet scene? That's something to avoid. I had enough of that with mom and dad. Take Kelly.

She won't go.

Go yourself and get drunk and molest all the wives.

I can do better than that, John said.

And he did. I will always regret missing his performance.

John Irving drove out his driveway thinking of his father. He had dreamt about him, seeing his tall, well-built figure in his khaki trousers, dark blue wind-breaker, polarized aviators, and straw porkpie. The man had a taciturn, focused way about himself. But there was something John remembered the man saying in the dream, and he was not sure if his father had said it in real life. The man said, You've got to be true to the game.

Cruising past the fields, John seemed sure to himself that his father had said this once for real; in the dream, the man passed in front of sighing willow branches, everything green and dark green around him, the wind whipping up.

You've got to be true to the game.

John was suddenly struck by the realization that his father would have been a great fly fisherman and would have loved the sport. Why hadn't he taken it up?

Chagrined, he drove on over the hills, past the fields occupied by big rolls of hay, to a last hill where the country club was. He parked the green Cougar next to Mercedes with paint jobs as thick and sleek as wet seal skin. Catbirds called loudly around him as he followed the path to the clubhouse.

Inside were expensive people from all over, the whole Main Line and then some: Philadelphia, Yardley, Newtown, New Hope, New York. They dressed as he expected, acted as he remembered. This was not his father's club where he had played as a boy, but it was not much different, just newer.

He got a glass of wine at the bar and strolled out onto the patio. The first few flights of golfers were coming in. People clapped for them—sweaty men and women in polo shirts, khaki pants, and leather shoes so tic-tacked with detail and studded with spikes they looked like crocodile heads. The return and scoring of the golfers was going to last several hours. John looked around and spotted a fellow in a blue club blazer. He stopped the young man and asked where the President of the club was. The young man escorted John over to an umbrella-topped round table on the patio. John went up to an older man with wispy grey hair who was dressed also in a blue club blazer. He said, Mister Danby?

The man turned from looking through the trees to face John. Yes? the old man said, screwing up his eyes through dark orange sunglasses.

I just wanted to say hello to you, sir. I'm a guest of a club member.

The man took off his sunglasses and stared, mouth open. Mister Irving, the man said slowly. It's so good to see you again. The old man rose and shook John's hand. It was so good of you to inscribe those books I sent you. Thank you so much. I'm sorry I didn't immediately recognize you there.

That's all right. We didn't pass much time that day in the library, John said. But I'm in town visiting my sister again.

Are you staying for the banquet then?

Of course.

You must sit at my table, Mister Irving.

Call me John, please.

What are you drinking there?

A little wine.

Did you get it from the bar there?

Yes.

The man scowled. I've better stuff in my study, Danby said. But first, let me introduce you.

Bucks County Club President Nathan Danby proceeded to introduce John Irving, the great American novelist, to bankers, lawyers, golfers' wives, club board members, old retired brokers who resembled Ivan Boesky and Roy Cohn, and their faded trophy wives. He introduced John to one chic young couple, the man dressed in riding clothes, the woman in a pleasant green dress that forced cleavage onto the innocent viewer. The woman said, Oh, Mister Irving, I read *The Hotel New Hampshire* my freshman year at Sweetbriar, her Virginia accent pronouncing "Hahmpshi-ah," and "Sweetbri-ah." Oh, I loved that novel, Mister Irving. If I had my copy, I'd ask you to sign it.

He signed my collection, Danby interjected.

Do you ride, Mister Irving? the tall, dark-haired boyfriend asked.

No. I wrestled.

Oh, the man said, smiling.

Danby led John to his upstairs study where he opened a bottle of Montrachet and poured John a glass. I'd ask a bartender to do it, he said, but I'd be afraid he'd break the cork there.

John and Danby settled into leather chairs. The old man launched into dozens of questions about how John wrote, what made him write, how hard or easy it was to work, and what he had planned next. John answered

THE MIDNIGHT FISH AND OTHER STORIES

politely and dutifully, answering with a surety as if he had he been asked about his fishing. Danby was entranced.

Well, listen, Danby said. I've got tons of guests and my wife is out there without me and I know she'll have too much to drink and fly off the porch there, so let me go. But when we get seated for the banquet, come to my table. I'll square it with...who did you say?

Brent Bilter.

Bilter, Okay then.

The two men went back down to the great patio. Before they parted, John asked Danby a favor, and Danby nodded, saying, That would be lovely if you said a few words tonight, then the old man walked off.

John took a seat next to the nicest-looking woman he found who seemed to be alone. She said, You're the writer, John Irving?

Yes. That's me.

I've not read a single one of your books so I suppose we've nothing to talk about, she said.

We could talk about you.

She shook her head. You're looking for material for another book, aren't you?

No, certainly not.

She smirked at him.

Is your husband out golfing?

My ex-husband is in Florida somewhere.

Golfing?

Who gives a shit about golfing? the blonde woman said. The conversation died quickly from there. John excused himself, wandered around, made small talk about literature for several hours, which he was good at, then was pleased to walk into the high-ceilinged banquet hall. He saw Brent and Colin. He went over to them. Hey, guys, he said. I've been co-opted by your President.

52

Yeah, Brent said, quizzical. He seems to think you're someone important.

Well, I am. I fish.

Danby seems to think you're a writer.

That too.

The banquet was uneventful. John made small talk with Mrs. Danby, Danby himself, and other septuagenarians around him.

In the time between the main course and dessert, Danby went over to a podium in the corner and addressed the crowd briefly, telling the golfers how well they played and what a great success the Invitational was. Then Danby said, We also are hosting a great guest this evening, someone who brings to this club a sense of honor and achievement, Mister John Irving.

At this, John stood, people turned to him and clapped. John nodded then sat.

Danby said, I'd like to ask Mister Irving to say a few words to us tonight, just by way of remembering this occasion then. Mister Irving?

John shook Danby's hand on the way to the podium, then turned into the microphone. He was a little giddy, but the tableaux of faces was so wide-spread and multi-hued he felt as if he were addressing a mural mute and harmless. The only movement out there among the white table cloths were the servers darting this way and that.

John began, Thank you, Mister Danby. It was a pleasure to meet you again today. Hello, ladies and gentleman.

John paused. He sought Colin and Brent. He saw them. He said, I would like to say a few words to you tonight about the greatest sport in the world, the most hallowed, superior sport that rises above all other pursuits. That sport, ladies and gentlemen, is fly fishing.

A barely perceptible ripple of air passed to the back of the room, reflected and came back.

Yes, John said, fly fishing. Fly fishing is an art, a pure art that connects you directly with the wild heart of a beautiful wild animal. Nothing else in the world does that. Nothing else surpasses that.

I could give you descriptions of the beautiful scenery and go on for hours about the solitude. Those are lovely, important parts of it, but the essence of the sport is based on distinct and incomparable pleasures: the deception of the fly and its presentation, the hook-up and battle, and the claim or release of the quarry.

John steadied himself at the podium. He listened to the audience. He heard them breathing.

He said, The fly has to be just right. Whether or not you tie it yourself, you have to make a choice based upon all your authority. Then you must make a cast, a cast that lands just right, in the right place with the right timing. Then you must make that fly act right, whether you must mend the line to prevent slack, or strip the line to make a streamer fly swim. In essence, you must perform. You must act out a fraud of nature using hand, rod, line, and fly.

You are connected, he said, and sometimes that fish runs out so much line you think it is pulling a string that will unravel your soul. This fight is conducted over the trembling, communicating live wire of the fishing line, through which you feel the very beat of battle, and feel the beat of a creature's heart as it stakes its will against your art. You realize that pound for pound this fish fights harder than you can.

John paused. The audience was still; they faced him, listening.

He said, Then comes the encounter itself. And so comes the highest requirement of fly fishing—the requirement of being rightfully moral. You can decide to let a fish go. You can declare that the fight is enough, that the fight is all you desire and that the fish has reaffirmed its wild freedom through its fight. But, if you are fishing for food, and intend on taking fish, then the responsibility is upon you to kill with grace. Not to leave a fish in the creel to suffocate, but kill it dead in the blink of an eye. The fish's beauty and greatness calls upon you to act just so and no less, if, in fact, you wish to eat.

Either way arises a great pleasure. Either the pleasure of setting the fish free to fight another time, or the pleasure of being a proper predator that kills cleanly for food and then has the pleasure of enjoying that food and enacting his or her role in the scheme of predator and prey.

This is visceral, true, and real, and greater than any abstraction played with clubs and ball. It affords an encounter with a wild thing.

Fly fishing is greater than golf, he said. Why? Because it is an extension upon life. It is an expression that is a double of life. It is a play upon the living acts of eating, fighting, and surviving. It is a combination of artifice, mechanics, and philosophy—fly, line, rod, reel, cast, presentation, morality of fighting and ending a fight—that is a graceful way of bridging worlds, air and water, of breaking through vision, yours and the fish's, and connecting pulse to pulse by a means designed to amplify and attune that connection.

John raised his head and looked out over the heads of the audience. He said, Fly fishing makes you realize your soul.

He stopped. The room was as silent as a church save for the hum of air conditioning, though the air was muggy.

But golf? he said. What connection to life does golf

have? What great connections does it create? When you swing a driver or connect with a chipping wedge, what essence of the soul is replicated and returned to you? What instincts are fulfilled—not just the instinct to compete and make a good shot, but the instinct fulfilled by creating a moment of art within nature, of breaking through the threshold of water with an extension of body and mind?

You golfers compete on a falsified field, the grass green because of chemicals, the land shaped just so because the earth has been engineered, the grass mown. You are daunted by the notion, the sheer, absurd notion, that with four of five swings of a metal prosthesis you shall put a small, white rubber ball into a perfectly round hole some distance away.

John cleared his throat. He looked at his hands which weren't shaking, then looked up. Some of the faces of the mural were pale, others twisted, a few stony and unlikable. He said, I suppose you do this because others do it. And you also do it for money, sometimes very big money. We fly fishermen may make our friendly wagers, but by its sheer nature fly fishing is impermeable to the multi-thousand-dollar purses some of you golf for because to pure angling money means nothing.

John rose to his full height, puffed his chest, and said, So stay with your hybrid of pinball and croquet. Bet the house on it. Continue to live a pursuit wholly false and falsified. Fly fishing does not want you. Once you ever touch a fly rod and look down upon a stream, your act of golf will be forevermore lessened and made more obtuse without having taught you anything. A fairway has no messages as does a stream. A hole in one is dumb luck, not the excellent stroke of a slack cast in the wind. The goal of golf, a low score, a scribble of numbers, is lost homework. A fish in the net is a living cache of jewels.

John paused, nearly spent, then added, Thank you.

The silence hung for a moment. No one stirred. Mrs. Danby clapped politely once, then twice, then stopped. The room was as silent as a crypt.

John went back to his table and sat down. The gallery of elderly faces peered at him in confusion. Slowly sound filled the banquet hall again with the mechanical dings and ticks of silverware and China. People whispered. Finally, Danby turned to John and said, Mister Irving, I don't think that kind of talk was appreciated here.

John nodded sagely. He said, I saw the need to make a statement.

It was surely not appreciated, Mister Irving, Danby said.

The wait staff was bringing out dessert, and John decided to slip out amid the movement of this last course. He said, It was an honor to sit with you tonight, Mister and Missus Danby. The old couple looked at him blankly. He said, I hope the rest of the tournament is wonderful as I'm sure it will be. John smiled. The people around him did not smile. As servings of peach cobbler landed on the table, John stooped and went along the wall.

When he turned at the windows he stood full and happy, looking into the crowd that sat stonily and appeared discolored as if they had been rained on. He tried to pick out his father's profile and fleetingly saw it as faces turned to look at him then look away, but, no, the man was not there. John chuckled.

As he went past the last table he saw Brent and Colin. They did not look up at him. He jogged over to them and patted them each on the shoulder. He said, Thanks for the invite, guys. I had a great time. Both golfers and their wives looked up aghast, without speaking. The others at their table said nothing. John, in one last, terrible blow, said, I hope I see you guys out there again on the river. Give me a call. Then he turned and went out the opened doors to the hallway. As he went through the lobby he swiped a handful of cigars from a humidor then went out the front as a club fellow in blue-blazer held the door for him.

Spring peepers and crickets called his way along the cement walk. He revved the Cougar and slowly drove past the sloped fields. When he shut down in his driveway he sat there. He felt as if he were filled with ether. He nodded off. He awoke to the sound of deer moving through the yard. He looked at his watch: 2 a.m. He got out of his car and went to bed.

When he was finished telling the story he blew a huge blue cloud of smoke from the Avo he puffed. I turned down what he offered me because cigars make me green. John smoked happily.

Do you think they recorded you? I said.

He shook his head. Doesn't matter. I remember what I said.

What possessed you?

It was the speech I always wanted to give. You've got to be true to the game, which means you've got to explain to yourself why you should be.

I can't believe they didn't throw you out.

Chickens.

That's because they thought you were John Irving, I said.

I am John Irving, John said.

True, I said, nodding, and sipped my powerful Daiquiri.

I only wish dad could have heard me. I think I finally would have made sense to him.

You think?

Yeah, he said, nodding, I do.

At least you remember most of the words, I said.

Yeah, John said, blowing a billow of smoke.

What happens now? I said.

John shrugged.

For a while nothing did happen. Brent and Colin did not call. John and I fished the little blue-winged olive hatch into early October. We caught trout in the streams, then on the river we fished baby shad imitations under the duns and hooked smallmouth and schoolie stripers. Leaves began to fall off the trees and decay, filling the air with the sweet-sour odor of early fall.

We went to Creighty's on a Saturday to buy stuff to tie flies over the winter. Old Creighty said, Where're those two pigeons you sent me, Irving boy?

They haven't been in here? John said.

Haven't seen them since July. I hope they didn't drown.

No, John said. They're dedicated golfers.

Creighty nodded, huffing, Oh.

Brent and Colin, chagrined at their very own club, spent every hour they had golfing, making par, being seen, buying drinks, going to parties, anything they could to make themselves look like full-fledged club members to disavow everything their guest, the great novelist John Irving, had said. Their putting got mushy.

That was not all that happened. Handicaps went up by the end of that summer at the Bucks County Country Club. More people were taking golf lessons than in years before. Thousands of dollars were spent by

club members on new equipment by Labor Day weekend. More of the men were thinking about seeing a psy-
chiatrist for reasons that were not readily connected to
golf but which drew upon frustrations that affected their
swing.

Therein was one man's assault on an American pas-
time. John Irving put a very dent in human experience
on Earth.

Just before Halloween, John called me. He said, Jesus
Christ, Len—Danby's hitting me up for the books I
signed.

You're kidding?

No. He sent me a bill for $1,300. Can you believe
that?

No shit?

He says if I don't pay him, he'll sue for more and
turn me in for forgery.

You better pay him, I said.

Goddamn old bastard, John said. I guess I'd better.
Damn, I wanted to get a 12-weight.

Right before Thanksgiving, John called me again. He
said, Len, you won't believe this.

What? I said. I heard John wrinkling paper.

He said, I got a letter from a lawyer. John Irving's
lawyer.

John Irving?

The one who's not me.

What's it say? I said.

It says I'm not supposed to impersonate Mister John
Irving anymore, ever again at any function, public or
private, et cetera, or else they'll sue.

Call him up and tell him it was a misunderstanding, I
said.

What should I do if I call him and find out he's a golfer? John said.

There is only one John Irving, and he fly fishes.

Damn right. We don't know who this other guy is, John said.

No, we don't, I said.

But if he's a golfer, he's wrong.

FIVE

The Fishing Son

Franklin Godwin had not ever caught a trout, or any other gamefish. He had caught two fish in his life: a carp, and an eel. He never mentioned these fish.

He lied about a lot of other fish. He had caught none of these fish, though he had many of them in his possession at one time or another. He came back into town with fish in his creel and showed them to people. He and his wife, Elaine, ate some, and he gave some to her parents, to neighbors, and to his mother who lived down river in Lambertville.

Franklin began fishing because he believed he had to. He knew this when his father died.

His father, Walton Godwin, had been in a wheelchair for most of Franklin's childhood. They lived in Carlisle, Pennsylvania, then, where his father had grown up and where Franklin was born. Polio killed Walton Godwin when Franklin was 10 years old. But while the man had been alive, he had told Franklin all about the fishing he had done on the Susquehanna and the Yellow Breeches. He had caught big smallmouth, wild brown trout, and mean, toothy pike, all on flies.

He was a big trout, going to wrap my line around a sunken tree down there, but I knew what he was thinking...

Franklin had no idea how tall his father had been. In

photographs, the man was much taller than his wife. He was wide-shouldered, big-headed, and sat stiffly in his wheelchair usually, but was more like a man resting easy when he told fishing stories. Franklin learned how and when to carefully approach the man and ask for stories. It was not easy to enter the downstairs room where his father spent all of his time. Franklin forcing his way through the hard shell of silence was not easy. Sometimes his father did not turn around to look at him. Other times, at night, Franklin heard all the way from his bedroom upstairs the shouts and cries of his father, and the sound of his fists pounding down on the wooden armrests of his chair.

But in the right atmosphere, Franklin got the stories he asked for. He often heard the same stories: the two big largemouth bass from a farm pond; the brown trout from the limestone creek; and the smallmouth from the Susquehanna.

There were a few black and white photographs from those days that confirmed what his father told him. In one, his father, seated on the back porch, holds a big largemouth bass. Another photograph, since misplaced, was one of a picnic scene in which his father, dressed in slick chinos and a checkered shirt, pulls a trout out of a creel. Franklin, who was three and four years old when the photos were taken, barely remembered the man who was photographed. In these pictures, Franklin's father seemed bold, capable, and most of all, happy. He was neither bold nor capable while Franklin knew him, and only fleetingly happy.

In reflection of his memories, Franklin told all his father's stories as if they were his own. At the university, in the National Guard, in the barracks and on the bus, and in his classes for his master's degree at the teacher's college, he told anyone who would listen about his fishing exploits. He told about the trout and the bass, the big smallmouth, and made up a few based upon his father's more apocryphal tales of pike. He moved like his father in story-telling gestures as his brown eyes lit up and he ran his hands through his amber hair when getting to an exciting part. He was tall like his father, thick but not fat.

Eventually Franklin had to catch up with his own lies. He perhaps had told them to force himself to do something about them. He used part of his Guard salary and money from his part-time bookstore job to buy rods, reels, and flies. When not with the Guard, and not in class at the college, he went fishing. And he was terrible.

He spent an entire afternoon whipping coils and coils of fly line into an indecipherable web. He was not very good at tying knots. Deciding that fly fishing was for experienced anglers, he went to prove himself first with a spinning outfit. He then cast plugs into the bushes. When he finally did place casts in the water, he lost spinners and jigs on sunken branches he thought were striking fish. He cast a plastic worm into another man's face.

Few people had actually witnessed Franklin's miserable attempt to fish. He had purposefully gone to places along the river where he saw no one. The hapless birdwatcher who took the plastic worm in the face was from out of town, and the slap of the worm knocked his glasses off and he did not see clearly the face of the person who apologized and scampered away.

On free weekends Franklin slipped off early in the morning to places along the river he hacked his way to with a bush knife. He wore his father's old hemp Lanson dress hat because that was what his father had worn fishing and because it fit well. He had bought a very good spinning outfit and fly rod and he worked at them both. As the summer passed, he improved: with a slow, fluid lash of his arm he sent out spinners and spoons, and with an excellent switch of the rod he loaded casts on his Fenwick fly rod and sent out streamers and poppers into pools and alongside rushes of water. Yet into late fall, and through the following spring, Franklin caught nothing. Breaking down one day he finally fished a worm on the bottom and caught a carp, a big, tugging, disgusting fish that he unhooked with the pliers. A few weeks later came the eel, an even more pernicious fish that lashed about Franklin's feet like a live wire, smearing him with slime as he chased it with the knife to cut the line. By this time he had begun to curse a lot, and had to be careful with his language because he had taken a job as a vice-principal of the Hunterdon Elementary School.

Franklin was in a jam. Everyone in town had seen him with fishing rods as he walked from his mother's house down to the river, or drove his big Nash down Main Street with rods visible through the windows. No one had seen him with fish.

Then he met Elaine Ikehoff and things got worse. Worse for fishing only, because Elaine was one of those healthfully pretty small town girls who know how to act in public and around older folks, but alone with boyfriends have a kind of happy zest that thrills men who, like Franklin, are virgins into their mid-twenties. Elaine, in fact, was more with the times, seemingly a hippy if her brown hair had been a little longer, her jewelry bigger. She worked across the river, in New Hope, as the secretary for an interior decorator. She had known who Franklin was since high school. She had been two grades behind him and had a crush on him. He had no idea who she was until one day in line at the bank on Bridge Street she looked behind her and there was Franklin. He wore dungarees and a hat. She said, That's a nice hat.

Franklin looked at her and saw her green eyes. His heart expanded.

As love goes, however, love for Elaine brought a different set of fishing concerns. When she took him to meet her parents up on the hill above town, Elaine's father recognized him as a man who fished. Elaine's mother exclaimed, Well, Franklin, you must catch us some fish. My mother taught me the most wonderful fish dishes, but Ben there—she pointed at her husband—he doesn't have the patience to fish. You must catch some.

Franklin glanced at his girlfriend who smiled and shrugged. Franklin was stuck. He had to produce more than stories now. His girlfriend, who he wanted to marry, and her father and mother sat there at the dinner table staring at him, waiting for him to speak. So he said, Okay

What was wrong with his fishing he did not know. He was sure that by the law of averages a fish eventually had to strike his lure, that the hook had to bite, the fish was to be landed, and it would be a keepable, edible gamefish, something to take a photograph of. But this had not happened after nearly a year of steady fishing. Franklin had gotten by on very well-placed lies, stories with just enough detail. Several times he drove all the way down to the next county where he found young boys from Trenton fishing the stocked trout in the canal and he bought fish off them. For four weeks in the spring of 1968 he drove down to the bridge over the canal near the Villa Victoria school and bought fish from the boys there, catfish and largemouth bass mostly. He drove his false catch back to Lambertville where he froze some for later, showed off a few and eventually gave them all to Elaine's mother for Saturday night dinners. During the April shad run, there were so many fish in town, all he had to do was be seen in proximity to the big, silver shad in buckets of ice. His reputation seemed assured, at least for this late spring when all else in the world was terrible.

Summer came, and he knew he was not able to buy fish off the kids for long. Of the remaining fish he had in the cooler in his mother's house he wrapped two or three in wet maple leaves, put them in a plastic bag, and buried them in the ground before he left for work in the morning. When he came home from the school, he surreptitiously exhumed the fish then made sure his neighbors saw him go out with his gear and waders, and made sure they saw the fish upon return. Up and down Clinton Street he was becoming renowned. People always asked him, Franklin, why don't you just set up a line right off your backyard? because the canal ran behind his mother's house. Franklin always told his neighbors that part of the excitement of fishing was getting away from home. He remembered his father always said that.

Then the frozen fish ran out. He was faced with a fishless summer while people talked about the fat smallmouth men and boys pulled out of the waters below the wing dam. Retired men came home from the shore with stout bluefish. Franklin started to get edgy.

He hit upon an immediate solution and asked Elaine to marry him. He wanted to marry her, and she wanted him to ask her. Franklin said he wanted to get married right away and Elaine's heart beat with the sudden fervor her man showed. They had had a glorious spring and early summer slipping away into the fields and woods. But how good marriage was going to be, because marriage meant, above all, that they would have to get a house that was full of privacy. With such impending pleasure, and also the business of organizing a sudden wedding, Franklin was excused from much fishing. The only unexpected glitch was that he was called up by the Guard for riot training. He trained for a week and came home with a terrible cough from the tear gas and his discharge papers.

Franklin and Elaine were married on August eighteenth in the Presbyterian Church, then had a catered dinner under a tent in the quiet, picturesque backyard of her parents house on the hill. The next morning they left by airplane from Philadelphia for a honeymoon to Miami Beach paid for by Elaine's parents and Franklin's mother. In Miami, on the sand, they forgot about the rest of the world.

When they returned from their honeymoon, they lived in what had been the guest room in Franklin's mother's house. Elaine and Franklin's mother, Betty Godwin, got along very well.

One night Franklin stayed up late to go through some papers from his school office. He sat at the desk downstairs. When he noticed the pink shape of his mother's dressing gown he looked up and saw her standing in the door to the hallway. They said goodnight. The woman lingered a moment, smiling. Then Franklin blurted, Mom? How come you never remarried?

Her eyes focused. She leaned against the molding and put her hands in the pockets of her gown. She said, I just couldn't imagine myself being married again. I guess I didn't want to go after anything big ever again.

But we moved away, Franklin said. We came here and you got this house. You got a job. I thought we started all over?

We did, the woman said.

Franklin had always assumed that his mother wanted to remarry and just hadn't found the right person. He figured she was still looking; she was only forty-eight. You just didn't fall in love with anyone? he said.

You sound as if you've given up on me.

No, he said, I haven't.

You're funny, his mother said, and waved goodnight. She walked up to her room.

Soon after, Franklin showered and went to bed. Elaine was asleep next to him. He tried to relax his whole body. He tried to leave go all sense that he controlled his legs and arms. He let his body sag. What may have otherwise felt relaxing and quieting to him felt leaden, heavy with the knowledge that stillness was sometimes a disease. He felt a near sense of dread. How had his father endured it, the physical awfulness of it, knowing long endurance led to slow death? He tried to recall if his father went mad in the end. No memories or images fit that notion. One day his father had simply been moved from the wheelchair to the bed in the same side room, downstairs. He lay in the bed as silent and stiff as a wooden man. Franklin though of himself laying in bed, in his father's place, his leaden body killing him with its immobile weight.

He refused this morbidity. Again, his father sat before him, a big man in a crisp, clean-smelling white shirt and necktie. The man had insisted on dressing properly no matter that he was not going anywhere. His big face moved, the cheeks, eyes, lips, and brow shaping the words and emphasis for every detail of every passage of every story.

I twitched that popper just once, and let it sit, and sit, and then I twitched it again and that big fish was coming...

After three months in his mother's house, Franklin and Elaine qualified for a mortgage from New Jersey National Bank and bought a home upriver in Stockton. They moved in a week before Christmas, decorating with what few pieces of furniture they had. They bought a massive Christmas tree and as many decorations as they were able to afford. The decorated tree overwhelmed the sofa. They spent Christmas Eve tucked on the sofa under a pile of blankets. Elaine said it was like sleeping at the foot of a mountain.

Winter was Christmas every weekend. Spring brought Franklin's wife-intoxicated mind back to the only bad reality of life: fishing. He had managed to avoid going fishing with men who invited him to the reservoirs, or to the shore—he pleaded school work or newlywed plans. And he avoided going to waters where there were serious fly fishers, like the Musconetcong and the South Branch. The charade was not going to last long.

Franklin sat at his desk in the main office of the school wondering to himself what he was going to do. He was not going to get away with buying fish from kids for a second season in a row. He was surprised the story hadn't gotten back to him the first time he did.

He wondered if he gave off special vibrations that only fish sensed; vibrations down his arms, through his hands into the line that gave off a signal in the water that drove the fish away. He tried to get his doctor to prescribe pills, saying he detected a shake in his hands. His doctor, an older fellow with orange hair, said he saw no signs of shaking and would not make a prescription.

The old doctor said, Franklin, if you're a little frazzled from a day at school have a shot or two of brandy. It'll do you fine. Franklin went to the local liquor store and bought a bottle of brandy but drinking it gave him an upset stomach. At the suggestion of the store owner, big Billy J, he tried flavored brandies, blackberry and apricot, and they were worse. He tried bourbon and nearly vomited. Elaine bought some white wine and it went down nicely, stayed down and didn't roil his stomach. He had several glasses one afternoon before he went fishing. This made him tipsy and he fell in the shale and hurt his knees.

What if there was no shake in his hands? What if he were fine, his casting fine, his presentation fine, his working the plugs or casting fly lines all fine? Had he somehow entered into an unending mathematical equation that kept fish away from him? Every time he went fishing, the turn of his lure, the swim of the fish, and the pull of the current all acted in contest? What if?

As he brooded on this fact one late spring afternoon in '69 he suffered a sudden spasm of anger and lashed the fly line until he had a pile of coils around him like wet spaghetti. He whipped and cut the coils with mad strokes of the rod, splashing all around. Then he stopped, breathless. He staggered up the river bank to the railroad tracks along the canal. He felt hopeless. Terrible and incredible things were happening in the world, and his predicament meant little, he realized, but he still felt badly. The government was going to put a man on the moon. They were going to work their way through all those equations and progressions and the curses of variables and drag. Yet somehow Franklin Godwin was unable to overcome the fishless progression he himself was in. He stumbled along the railroad tracks beside the canal, dragging green line behind him.

He watched his plodding feet in the boots of his waders. They were covered in wet gray mud that was dusted with fine, glittery gray dust from between the railroad ties. Then before him he saw another pair of boots pointing at his.

Franklin suddenly looked into the face of a short, wiry man in his fifties or sixties. The man had a bold, tanned face that was wrinkled but strong, with a tough, flat little nose and small blue eyes behind big horn-rimmed glasses. His head was covered with salt-and-pepper gray hair buzz-cut with a short tuft left standing in the front. He wore chest waders that had been cut down so they ended at his lean middle and were held with narrow leather suspenders. The man wore a green army sweater over a white T-shirt, and carried a canvas satchel over his shoulder and a net strung from the garrison belt that pulled tight his waders. He had a bamboo fly rod in his right hand. He seemed to have landed there where he stood, like a bird.

The man said, You're that National Guardsman who fishes, aren't you?

Yes, goddamnit, that's me, Franklin groaned.

Watch your language, the man said. He looked Franklin up and down. You haven't caught a thing all day today, have you?

Franklin shook his head no.

Why, you haven't ever caught a thing at all, have you? the man said, his eyes bright and his mouth wide with the words.

Yes, Franklin said, forlorn, legs tired. I just haven't. I never have. I just can't. He sat down on the rail and held his head in his hands. I don't know why, he said. I just can't.

The man looked down at him. He said, You better stand up, a train's coming.

Franklin looked southward down the tracks and saw the misshapen black oval and bright white dot, the image wavering in the heat. He got up and both he and the old man stepped down the canal bank until they were ankle-deep in the brown water.

The old man said, What about the fish you've come into town with?

I got them from people, Franklin said, sagging, his body shocked at the loss of the weight of the charade. It's all over now, he thought. He sat on the grass, his feet in the canal, his body feeling made of straw. Grasshoppers flickered over him.

The older man nodded. He looked down the tracks at the approaching train. The rails began to hum near the two men; the sound of the train in the distance was indistinct. The train horn blew and the old man waved with his hand holding the fly rod. He looked down at Franklin and said, I can help you, and then the train was nearly there. Franklin was distracted by the noise and said, What did you say? As the freight train rumbled past the man said again, I can help you, but his words were pounded by the great clashing and squeals of metal at forty miles an hour yards away. Franklin looked up at the small, black-outlined form, the man's back against the sun that lit the short hair on his head like a halo of quartz. The man seemed to be talking with the force of the train, his words utterances of axles and clasps. The man spoke and nodded. Franklin looked at him, expressionless. The man nodded again. Franklin shrugged and nodded his head.

When the train passed it sucked away all sound for a moment. In the silent vacuum the old man said, You need me to help you.

What?

I can catch fish and give them to you. You can say

you caught them. Easy. See?

Franklin didn't know what to say. He blurted, You'll keep it a secret?

I wouldn't offer if I couldn't keep my mouth shut.

Why the hell are you suggesting this?

No curse words, please. I don't like cursing.

Sorry, Franklin said.

The old man sat on the grass next to him. Franklin looked at the man's hands. They were liver spotted and tan, hard, the veins seemingly soldered onto scoops of steel that were fashioned into hands. The man said, I've never not caught fish. Been at it for a long time.

Franklin noticed that the man did not wear a wedding band or college ring. He looked at the ring on his own finger. Franklin said, You ever married?

The man jerked with a silent laugh. He said, Yeah. Once.

My wife believes me completely. She's the one that bothers me the most. I'm lying to her.

The man studied Franklin a moment, his eyes scanning down the young man's face. The older man nodded, looking at the canal.

Why do you want to help me? Franklin said

The man cocked his head and looked at Franklin who found it difficult to return the stare of those goggly blue eyes enlarged by the horn-rimmed glasses. The man said, I like fishing. I like to catch fish. I like to set up a challenge for myself. I've done this before. You need to catch fish. I'll catch you the fish. Gives me something to aim at.

And you won't tell?

Nope. And you won't tell.

What do I give you in return? Do I pay you?

You can just cover my expenses. Say ten bucks a pop. But you know what I really want you to do?

What?

I don't want you to ever catch a fish.

No?

No, and I mean not ever. When you go out fishing, don't cast at all. Just sit in the trees. Or if people go with you, bend back the hooks. Don't hook a fish, ever. Don't bring one in yourself.

Why not? Franklin said.

That's just our deal.

It'll be pretty easy to keep, Franklin said.

It better be, because if you catch a fish, someone will die.

What?

Someone will die.

Get out of here.

Don't you think a man who catches fish like I do knows things? Don't I?

Sure.

The man said, Then I know—if you ever catch a fish somebody's going die. You'll know 'em too.

Come on, Franklin said, incredulous.

The man nodded emphatically. You listen to what I say, he said. You want this deal, you want to go on being known as one of the best fishermen around here, then you make this deal with me and you never ever catch a fish yourself. Not on your life. The man's head bobbed with emphasis on each word and his eyes flashed.

The way the man spoke these last words made Franklin worry that it would be himself who died if he caught a fish, and that the lean, fierce man might be the one who kills him. Who was this guy? Franklin recognized him but wasn't able to place him. He knew he had seen him around. Deep down Franklin knew this man was serious and should be taken that way, and the offer might be all right. The man had a funky scent of leather, beer breath and day-old shirt, and the cast of his face and eyes all lent a credence to him. But nothing was more certain than the touch of his steel hand on the fly rod: light, deft, just playing with it, making a Woolly Bugger perform a jig in the surface tension of the slow canal.

Franklin shook the man's hand on the deal. The man gave Franklin his telephone number and said to call him whenever he needed fish and then they would work out the details each time. Franklin asked the man his name. The man said, Call me Pete. Franklin introduced himself and the man said, I know.

They parted, Franklin walking away, the man moving further down the tracks, heading for the frothy run along the steep, rock-walled river bank.

With that began a partnership that was to sustain Franklin's charade. Whenever Franklin needed trout for his mother-in-law's table or a few good bass to show off at the liquor store, he called Pete. The man answered the phone after two or three rings and said his name. Franklin told him what he needed, and they designated a place to meet. Sometimes they met for the exchange of money and fish down a dead-end road in some trees, or in the parking lot behind a warehouse. The pond south of town at Belle Mountain was also an exchange location. They had to move around lest anyone begin to notice the regularity of their meetings. About once every two weeks they exchanged brown and rainbow trout, or smallmouth, largemouth, shad, and once an incredible pickerel. Franklin paid a flat fee of $10.

Beyond fishing, Franklin had absolutely no contact with the man. As they conspired into the new decade, Franklin had come to learn that Pete was in his mid-fifties, a bachelor, a semi-retired electrician who lived in a small white house on the north end of Lambertville, not far from where Franklin's mother lived. No one knew Pete very well, no one that Franklin spoke with. Pete kept to himself, was nice to his neighbors, kept his property neat, fished a lot, and was known to be drunk sometimes. People said he lived off family money.

One night in 1973, Pete delivered a magnificent brown trout that Franklin mounted and put on his den wall. He had people over to look at the fish, buddies from town. They toasted his health with wine and bourbon. They asked if he had pictures of the fish his father caught.

Ebullient, Franklin dragged out an old photo album to show his friends the only photographic evidence he possessed that confirmed his father had actually caught fish. Sandwiched among fuzzy black and white photographs of picnics and parties was a black and white eight-by-ten glossy, over-exposed, of his father sitting on a wicker chair on a porch with a nice largemouth hung from his hand:

The man is beaming, his teeth big and white. He wears a white dress shirt and a wide striped tie, his cigarettes in the front pocket. The Lanson hat is on the table next to him, where there are two beer bottles.

Franklin's friends asked what his father had caught the fish on. He told them his father used poppers he tied himself. The young men smiled. Franklin felt a strange clamminess as he heard his father's voice when he spoke.

A few days later he telephoned his mother. He said, Mom, where did all of dad's fishing gear go when he died? He wondered why he had not asked this question many years before.

I guess it was given away, she said.

You guess? Franklin said.

His brother must have taken some. I probably gave some away too.

Uncle Jim didn't fish.

I guess he gave the stuff to people. I really don't remember, Franklin. It was so long ago. It was such a mess.

Was all his fly-tying stuff given away too?

What did it look like?

Sort of a kit with a little vise, and bobbins and scissors.

If he had that I never saw it. I never would have seen that sort of thing.

Franklin's stomach was cold. He said to his mother, I was just thinking if some old equipment was laying around I'd restore it.

Well, I'm sorry, but it must have all gone with him.

They talked a while then said goodbye.

Franklin tried to remember if his father had shown him rods and reels and flies. Maybe the man had been embarrassed about ending up in a wheelchair and gave his equipment away.

In early June, one smoky night, they met in the orange flood-light of a parking lot by a warehouse outside Ringoes. When Franklin pulled up in his new VW squareback, he saw Pete leaning in a slouch against the side of his green LeMans. The old man slowly looked up so his eyes caught the glare of Franklin's headlights, and his eyes flashed behind the thick spectacles like wet orbs. Franklin got out and as he approached, Pete looked hard at the younger man and said, You know, you're a low down man for doing this and I'm a low down man for doing it too.

Franklin said nothing at first. Pete didn't smell of liquor and he didn't seem drunk. Franklin said, Why say that now? We've been doing this for four years.

You weren't out there tonight.

No. I was down in the park at Washington's Crossing going for a jog. That's what I've started doing, you know, when I'm supposed to fish.

Jogging?

Yeah. I feel pretty good.

Pete snorted. Gonna live forever, huh?

Franklin was about to reply but he suddenly remembered Pete's warning about ever going fishing: death for someone, possibly Franklin. He said, So what happened tonight?

It was one of those nights, Pete said. His narrow chest rose and fell. He seemed nearly sad. He put his key in the trunk of the car and opened it and the door light came on. In the yellow electric gleam Franklin saw a smallmouth that had to be eighteen inches long. It was beautiful.

Pete turned his back. He faced the warehouse as he spoke.

I was fishing the river at the Water Gap. The sun was getting low. Then I saw the big Drakes flying up high. On a crazy hunch I tied one on. I cast it to an eddy and it just floated there. I just did it so I could look at it. Trout fishing's been rough this year. Then he took it, Pete said, nodding back at the fish.

If you wanted to put him back you could have. It wouldn't matter if you didn't have any fish, Franklin said.

Pete turned his head and looked at Franklin. He said, Wouldn't you just once like to catch a fish like that?

Sure I would.

Well, you can't, cause we have a deal. I'm the fisherman. You're the public figure. Better take this one home. Show him off at the liquor store.

Franklin rummaged in his pocket for the cash.

Pete said, What if I told you this fish costs one-hundred dollars?

Then you can have him for your wall, Franklin said.

Pete shrugged. He said, You can have him. He's priceless. What the hell could you pay for him?

Franklin felt sickly. He picked up the fish with his fingers in its gills and said, Well, then I'm sure as hell gonna spend the money to put him on my wall.

Pete nodded. Mmm-hmm, mmm-hmm, he hummed, nodding.

Franklin opened the hatch of his VW and put the big, cold bass in his creel. He shut the door.

Pete jangled his car keys in the pocket of his paint-crusted khaki pants. He said, I know you're going to take pleasure in showing off that fish tonight. I just want you to know I took greater pleasure in that fish. Pleasure you're not ever going to know. Pete steadied himself. He wished he hadn't kept the fish but had done so to make a statement to himself as much to Franklin. He kept it because he felt a drunk coming on and felt bitter, and didn't believe there was anything sacred in fishing anymore. There had been bigger smallmouth that he had let go, but he didn't know if he believed in the glory of fishing anymore and had tested himself to see if he cared. He did, he still cared, immensely, and hated himself for taking a fish not in the way a man keeps for himself a fish that he has caught, but for taking a fish to show up another man.

Franklin swallowed. Something about the way Pete spoke told him that the old man wasn't trying to intimidate or hurt, but was trying to make something clear.

Pete said, This is why we have our deal, you know?

How? Franklin said.

Pete said without sarcasm or meanness, Because a guy like you isn't ever supposed to know the real pleasure. The real sport. You're some guy who came into this sport because you put yourself up to it to impress others, and yourself. It wasn't handed down to you, man to man.

It sure as hell was, Franklin said, angry for the first time. My father fished. He caught fish like you've caught fish, probably even better.

Pete smiled a terrible smile. He said, Did he take you fishing?

No. He couldn't. He was crippled. He got polio. He died when I was a kid.

But did he ever put a rod in your hand?

No.

Why did you start fishing when you were a man?

Franklin shouted, Because I...because I said I could—his voice echoed off the corrugated metal side of the warehouse.

Pete said, You started because you probably told a story about yourself just like your father did.

Hell, no. Goddamn you. I taught myself to fish because of my father, he shouted.

Bad language, Franklin.

The hell with you, you old shit. You're pissed off because you've got a deal with me to catch my fish for me. That's all. Don't give me some guff about why I tried to fish. Fishing is in my blood.

If it were you'd catch fish.

What's that supposed to mean?

It means that I started this deal because I don't want someone like you to ever catch a fish. I don't want you to ever know the pleasure of the hunt and the fight, or the feel of keeping or letting them go. You misinterpreted something your daddy told you and if there's something wrong with you so you can't fish then there was something wrong with your old man too.

Franklin felt coldcocked. No one had ever spoken to him about his father this way. He wanted to jump on Pete and knock him down and kick him in the ribs. He stood in a lurch with his fists clenched. Pete continued to face him, apparently ready to take whatever Franklin might throw.

Franklin said, Don't ever mention my father ever again. He's not yours to talk about.

Until you catch fish you can't talk about him either, Pete said.

Franklin blinked.

Pete, his face slack, got in his car, started the throbbing engine, and drove away. Franklin stood in the empty space alone, a pale figure in the orange floodlight surrounding the warehouse.

He eventually pulled himself to his car, got in, and sat. He never felt more like crying since his father died. How dare this old bastard say such things? Franklin kicked the firewall, then started the VW and drove fast back to Stockton. He wheeled hard into a parking space on the street, grabbed the creel, and walked briskly into the liquor store.

The usual gathering was there: big, hairy Billy J, the owner, and five other men, all locals of Franklin's age, of various shapes and sizes, winnowing the last hours of a Thursday night. They rested upright, languid, near the counter in the middle of the room amid the sparkling bottles of liquor and wine. They hailed Franklin when he walked in, saying, What'cha got?

Franklin plunked the creel down on an unopened box of Wild Turkey, gently opened the lid and drew the fish out slowly. The men gasped and Billy J whistled then said, My god, we've got to get a picture of that.

Another man said, Use black and white. That prints better in the newspaper.

They all posed against a tall shelf of wine bottles and Billy J took a picture. The fish was weighed and measured, Franklin patted on the back the whole time. Billy J said, By god we need to have a toast on this, and he pulled out a bottle of George Dickel from the shop office. He poured each man a measure.

After the fish had gone into a bag of ice and the group of men was breaking up, the shop door opened at the very last minute of business hours. Someone said, Hey, there's Pete Johansen. Show him the fish, Franklin.

The bourbon burned inside Franklin's gut. Pete had driven up to the store on purpose.

Pete looked at no one as he nosed around until he found a big jug of Jim Beam and approached the counter with it. He seemed like a slightly bewildered, aging man who found he was out of whiskey.

Billy J said, Pete, you won't believe the smallmouth bass that Franklin caught. Show it to him, Franklin.

Franklin picked the bag of ice off the floor. The dark shape of the fish showed against the plastic. Franklin felt as if caught with the dead body of the President.

Nice one, Pete said. Where'd you get him?

In the river, Franklin said, dry mouthed.

Where specifically?

At the Water Gap.

Pete nodded. He paid for his liquor. There's a good taxidermist in Ringoes, he said. He went out the door.

The big bass caused some trouble for Franklin. A front page photograph with a short caption appeared in the *The Lambertville Beacon* newspaper. People telephoned him. People asked exactly where he had been. A fellow who wrote for *New Jersey Outdoors* saw the article and wanted to interview Franklin. Franklin offered to do the interview right then and there over the phone while the lies he had told were fresh in his memory. The details always had to match because numerous matching, exact details were the keys to a successfully repeated lie. He answered the man's questions then hung-up, his head spinning.

If Franklin and his wife had children, the secret would have been broken because a child is always suspicious when one or both parents are a fraud. But Franklin and Elaine had tried and not produced any boys or girls. They took this in stride. By then they had a half-breed Greyhound, a shy, pale animal, and a bigger brown dog of no clear heritage, the house protector.

At night Franklin brooded in his den, sipping white wine. Queenie, the greyhound, attended him. He was wondering if people were starting to figure out what he did. He felt as if a ring of people were closing in, a ring that was a part of the arithmetic progression he was locked in: the inability to fish leading to the desperation of lying to the paranoia of fraud. Where did it end?

As he lay in bed that night next to Elaine, Franklin mulled over his situation. He wasn't sure he was able to sustain it. He was tiring of it. He thought about telling Pete he wanted to stop. No penalty came with stopping, only with catching a fish. His mind wandered over the things Pete had said when he gave up the big bass then wandered into his father's voice talking.

I got lucky all the time. There wasn't a time I was ever not lucky. I had fishing luck...

Franklin suddenly sat up in bed. He slipped from under the sheet and went down to his den. He took out the photo album and flipped to the photograph of his father with the bass. He picked up a magnifying glass and under the desk light he put the glass over the chiseled shape on the edge of the photograph, another man who sat at the table. He saw stubbly hair on the side of the man's head, a high cheek bone.

The man in the photograph with his father was Pete.

The next morning during his lunch hour Franklin went to his mother's house. She wasn't home but he let himself in. He went to the living room shelves and opened the hinged glass door and took out the oldest photo album, one full of pictures from before he remembered. He turned a few pages and found nothing. At the back in a thick envelope were more photographs. He opened this and soon came across what he thought had been lost: a series of photographs from a picnic, a series that included the photograph of his father standing, holding the trout, a magnificent image. Then there was another photograph, a man holding a much bigger trout. This man was Pete, his face not as seamed and thin as Franklin knew it, but was the same severe countenance with its intense eyes so blue they were silver in the photograph.

Franklin slammed the album shut. He was queasy with shock.

He sat down in a chair. His body slackened and his hands shook. Why did his father know this fiendish little man? Did they fish together? Franklin felt a heavy sense of dread, as if he had walked in on a terrible moment in his family's life that he was not supposed to see. Why hadn't his mother ever spoken about this man? The answer was obvious: they had a relationship of some sort, kept secret, something important enough that Pete followed Betty Godwin from Carlisle to Lambertville.

Franklin began nodding to himself. Yes, this was who

Pete was—a phantom friend of his father's better days who had gone after that man's wife once that man was immobile. Franklin's mother was either ashamed, or intensely secretive, or both, to have carried on with this Peter Johansen while Franklin was growing up.

Why is he involved with me? Franklin wondered. What is he trying to do? Franklin was startled and angered. He looked at the photographs again. It was all there very plainly: his father, his mother, and Pete among them, in a group photo. Franklin gripped his shirt. He wondered what to do. He was unable to bring himself to confront his mother; that was too terrible to do.

Franklin left the house an altered man. He did not know what to do. There was nothing he was able to say to his mother. As for Pete, he felt he could crush the little man for insinuating himself into his father's life, and his mother's, and Franklin's own. But then Franklin didn't care. The man was a drunk fool with nothing better to do with himself. Summer was coming to an end. Franklin didn't have to fish anymore. He was going to walk away from the whole charade.

That's what it all was, some strange, morose charade: his father's stories, his mother carrying on with Pete and never speaking about it, and Franklin paying Pete for fish. It was too complicated to pick up and sort out. It was not to be bothered with.

A week later when Franklin came home from school, he stopped to sit on the porch and look through the mail. He listened to Elaine's footsteps in the house on the wooden floor. It sounded as if she walked in a circle. He realized she still wore her dress shoes. He went in and found her in the dining room. He raised his eyebrows at her and puckered his lips.

She said, I'm pregnant.

Franklin said nothing. He didn't move. He thought he misheard her.

She said, I'm pregnant. I went to the doctor today.

Franklin made a gurgling sound.

My period is almost three weeks late. I went to my ob-gyn. It didn't take her five minutes to figure it out.

Franklin exhaled and made a dog-like whimper.

We're waiting on the blood test but the doctor's positive about it, she said. She looked at him as if she had said something terrible, chin down, eyes peering at him. She said, Franklin?

The room grew larger and smaller but in the refraction of space he found his wife and kissed her and cheered then gasped. He stepped back and looked at her face. He looked at her breasts. He looked lower, at her small, slightly round belly. He started laughing. They kissed. Franklin said, But we couldn't?

Elaine looked at him with wide eyes. The doctor thinks that maybe most of my eggs were invalid, she said, but then this good one came bobbing down. She put her hands over her mouth as if what she said was an outrage.

Franklin wiped his brow. He and Elaine had long given up using birth control. Nature had out-foxed them. Franklin giggled. He ran to the refrigerator and pulled out a bottle of champagne they were saving. Then he looked at her and said, I guess you can't have any.

She said, It's okay. You go ahead.

Hey, you've had wine, he said.

I told my doctor and we figured out how much I had had, and she said she didn't think it made a difference. I usually had it with food. That's okay. Did I ever have a lot?

Not that I remember, he said.

Open the champagne, she said.

We'll save it for the day the baby comes.

No. Open it now. We should toast ourselves.

Jeez, we should, Franklin said, wiping his brow with the bandanna again. He uncorked the champagne and filled a glass. He told Elaine she had to have a sip and she did. Then he took a long, big, sizzling mouthful that went down with a hard swallow and felt very good. Wow, he said. He shook his head and slugged down some more champagne and kissed his wife. The dogs came in and looked at the two people and knew very well what was up.

That night Franklin and Elaine sat on the porch in the summer air. The light of several candles lit them. He looked at her where she sat in her chair. He said, I don't think my father fished at all.

I thought he did all the time? she said.

I can't find any of his old equipment.

I thought your mother said he gave it all away when he got polio?

Maybe. All I know is that when I started fishing, I went and got all new equipment because I couldn't find any in the house.

Stuff always disappears, Elaine said. Molly, the brown dog, put her head in Elaine's lap and Elaine stroked the dog's soft brow.

I don't think my father fished at all. I think he had someone do it for him.

Franklin, that's crazy, Elaine said.

He shook his head. He said, I think I know who did it.

Who?

This guy who my father knew, he said.

Elaine asked if he had proof. He said he had none.

She looked at her husband's broad, tanned face. She did not know what to tell him about how much he agonized over the past.

At the end of a quiet day in the school in September Franklin eased back in his swivel desk chair in his office. He dialed the phone. Pete answered. Franklin said, I need a big fish.

What kind?

I want two big bass like you caught for my father back in forty-nine.

There was a pause on the end of the line filled by the obscene sound of liquor washing down the man's throat. Pete said, I can't right now. Give me a week.

It was you, right?

Sure. It was me.

How?

I can't tell such a long story now.

Tell it, Franklin said sharply. You know you have to tell it.

Pete took another long sip of whiskey. He sighed. He said, All right. But how'd you figure it out?

You said something about my father the night you gave me the big bass. I thought about that. I looked in the family album. I saw you sitting with dad.

Yeah. That was me. He didn't have me around the house much. I once brought him some fish at a party he had. I think they were trout. I think someone took a picture of me then.

My mother took the photograph.

Yeah.

Dad could walk then. Why didn't he fish?

Wasn't any good at it. Didn't have any patience. But

we all lived not too far from the river, and your father knew a lot of men who fished. Men he did business with. He wanted to impress them. Easy as that. Same reason you did it. Pride.

Franklin squirmed in his chair. He said, What did my father give you in return?

Money. It was all right to get paid to fish. Fishing kept me dry mostly. I didn't do it for long.

What happened when my father got polio?

Pete breathed heavily as if worn-down by his own words. He said, I don't know. I wasn't around him. If he made up stories, who was going to call him a liar?

Franklin was chagrined. His chin was on his chest.

I don't think your mother ever knew, Pete said.

I had no idea either, Franklin said.

Listen, Franklin. Your father was a normal man. He wanted something. You know—Pete's voice grew deep as he drank more—you know, once I got liquored up and made a pass at your mother.

Franklin didn't want to hear this.

Pete said, I never had a chance with her. When he died and she moved away, I came to see her. I asked her to marry me. She said she couldn't. But I liked it around here, this part of the country. I moved here. Boy, I was after her. She never wanted much to do with me. She never told you about me either. She was a careful woman about you.

Franklin said, When you saw me on the canal bank, on the tracks that day, you knew who I was, didn't you?

Sure. When you said you hadn't caught anything all day, and I saw that hat, I figured you were as stupid about it as your daddy and didn't deserve to catch a fish. I was still angry, I guess. Angry at doing some wrong things. Mad I didn't get to marry your mother. I saw you and had you pegged for your dad. You look just like him. No reason for you to fish.

Franklin said, What about me catching a fish and someone dying?

Just something I said.

Why say someone was going to die?

Fishing killed your father, didn't it?

Polio killed him.

Now you're all full of stories just like him, Pete said.

Franklin said nothing. He hung up the phone. He intoned, *I lie because I was given a lie. If I catch a fish, someone will die.* It was a rhyme he had made up to stand as the last line to all the stories.

Franklin thought about his mother. There was nothing to say to her. He had found out some huge chunk of history and had to store it away. To ask her was to examine it all again was too much. She lost too much all at once, her marriage and her husband as well. No wonder she had been so shocked and dazed for nearly a year, sleeping and sagging her way through the weeks and months. It was not until Franklin was nearly in high school that she started going on dates with men. But she never seemed happy and never appeared attached to anyone. As a boy Franklin rarely saw any of these men face-to-face, and he did not recall ever seeing Pete, but at the time he knew they existed and he always doubted these men. He put them up against his belief in his father, and his father's memorial strength and success corrupted the character of any man who entered his mother's house.

He lay awake in bed at night thinking about his wife, the baby that was coming, and his own father and mother, and himself. These people hung over him like a funny cluster of stars. Somehow a line was to be drawn to connect them all, but he did not know what order to connect them. He felt no anger over his childhood, over all his young life before this very night; just disappointment.

Franklin went to see his mother one Saturday before Christmas. He said he was in town and wanted to say hello. She smiled at him from where she sat in her chair. He smiled, sitting on the sofa, sipping the tea she had made for him. He felt badly for her. He didn't want her to know that. He talked to her about Elaine. His mother was very happy about the baby.

Through the winter Elaine's womb grew and stretched her belly. In bed, Franklin palmed her melony sides to feel the baby kick. He liked to talk to the baby through Elaine's side. They had a small party, just the two of them, when they were past the sixth month.

By March, Franklin was shoving money into small investments and a few certificates of deposit. He let repairs to the house and car go by. Elaine and he found themselves in a kind of slow whirlwind.

On a quiet, cloudy evening in the new spring, Franklin stood in his back yard. He looked into the pages of his fishing log. He had recorded every fish Pete had ever caught and entered them in his neat, small script with a fountain pen. He had kept it in his fishing vest as a kind of epitaph. If for some reason he fell and hit his head or drowned while fake fishing, or died in a car crash, people would find the booklet and possess his false record that then would be forever his. He knew that was how he would die, if he had to die soon.

He stripped out the pages and dropped them in a battered steel bucket. He lit a match down in the bucket and touched it to the torn edges. Soon it all burned away. He felt his blood swishing through his body. He drove up to the Raritan River, fished, and caught nothing.

The following Wednesday he called Elaine from the school office. He asked if it would be all right if he went fishing after work. He wanted to sneak out when school was over. She said it was fine. The baby wasn't due for another two, maybe three weeks, but Franklin and Elaine had entered a state of soldierly readiness.

At the end of this day, Franklin went down to the detention room and saw three morose students sitting at the desks. He told the attending teacher she could leave, then he dismissed the boys, giving one of them a ride home. Then he raced to a spot near the mill house. He had put his gear in the VW the night before. He slipped off his wingtips and then tucked himself into his waders, still wearing his blue shirt and tie. He put on the hat, assembled the Fenwick, and walked out.

He was never to forget the spot because of the tree, a huge tulip tree amid smaller maples and sumacs. The tree stood out on a point of land and leaned slightly over a riffle of quick, shallow water. To the side of the riffle, just out of the shadow of the tree, was where the smallmouth struck.

A sharp jolt came down the line and the rod tip sprang and Franklin felt in his hands the electricity of the fight he had never felt before. The juice built up and down the line, in the rod, and filled up in his hands in a surge. The whippy rod bowed as the smallmouth ran across the current.

Franklin was dancing back and forth where he stood, having no idea what to do. He held the rod up, then turned it against the fish's short turns. He was nearly too in awe to make himself think what to do next.

The bass broke water, coming straight up. It flashed.

Franklin caught his breath. The fish landed on its side. He began to wind it in. It came. It jolted and thrashed a few times and made a few short runs, then Franklin had it close. He was amazed by this animal on the end of the line as he peered at its flickering form in the water nearby.

He swept it into the net. He looked in at the fish's small, sleek colorful body. Its gills opened and closed rhythmically as if it panted with exhaustion. Franklin scampered over to a flat, exposed rock. He sat on the rock and reached into the net and took the bass by the lower lip. He held it up. It was a dark golden brown with patches and stripes that lit up when he turned it at an angle. Its eye was like a bubble of blood with a black center. The fish weighed maybe a pound.

Franklin laughed aloud with mirth and success. Finally, he said. Finally, finally. He studied the little bass again then slipped it back into the water. The fish wobbled a bit then straightened, and it disappeared.

He paused for a moment and looked out over the water. That was it, then.

Franklin looked at his watch. He allowed himself five more good casts. Upon stripping in the fifth cast he sighed. That's all right, he said; it was all right to him that nothing else happened that day because everything was different then and there were many days to come. He went back to his car, pulled off the waders, put on his shoes and drove home.

When he got into the kitchen he saw Elaine sitting in the kitchen wearing her windbreaker. Her already-packed suitcase was beside her. She looked at him, pained and smiling. Let's go, she said. Franklin drove quickly to the hospital in Flemington, his fishing gear rattling in the back.

He checked Elaine in and she was rolled away in a

wheel chair. Franklin filled out forms then was directed to the waiting room. He waited for a long time, unable get a nurse to answer his questions. Finally a nurse came to him. She said there was trouble.

What trouble? Franklin said.

The baby is a breech. The doctor is trying to turn it and if not then we're going to do an emergency C-section.

Franklin was unable to speak for a moment.

The nurse said, She's hanging in there. Do you want to come in?

Franklin nodded. The nurse took him quickly to a small dressing room and handed him green scrubs then she ran off.

Franklin scrambled into the baggy clothes. His body felt slow and heavy. A nurse waved him down a short corridor and through a door. He walked into the delivery room.

Sound and odor hit him first. There were cries and gasps, Elaine's voice, and the shouts of the nurses and doctor. A machine beeped. Franklin smelled iodine and blood, and the strong odor of birth.

He went to Elaine and held her right arm. She clenched him with her hand. He looked at her. She appeared lit with white, wet fire. He said nothing. She cried and shook. The doctor shouted, Push now, push.

Franklin glanced around. He had never seen anything like this, not in the National Guard or anywhere else. This was for real, no fraud or practice fire. His breathing slackened. Elaine yelled in his ear.

The room began to tilt and only the grip of Elaine's hand held him down. He leaned over her. All he saw was the movement of blobs of color around him and Elaine's clear, ecstatic face close to his. A circle of grey closed around her face. He sat on the bed, sagging, and his forehead jolted against Elaine's wet face then he raised himself off his wife. As his sight returned, a shiny, sleek, many-colored newborn appeared between his wife's knees as if hovering there on its own.

Elaine did not pass out though much blood stained the floor at the foot of the bed. Half-delirious, she smiled at Franklin. Their baby, reddening in color, was given to them wrapped in white.

Days later Franklin and Elaine sat on the porch. The dogs lay next to their rocking chairs as Elaine nursed the baby. The three grandparents had invited themselves over for supper the third night in row. As Franklin studied Elaine and the baby boy, he possessed in himself for the first time a kind of quickening, as if his arteries and veins were wider and run with much more blood. He watched Elaine and the baby for an hour, then he drove down to Lambertville to get his mother. Before going to her house, he drove to the liquor store on North Franklin street to get some beer for his father-in-law.

When he parked the car at the curb, he sat there a moment. The pulse in his veins slowed when he saw Pete come out of the liquor store.

He watched the older man move down the sidewalk; the man walked smoothly, but the look on his face was that of someone not certain which way he was going next. Franklin watched him through the back window of the car. He wanted to jump out and grab this man and shake out of him every story about his own father that the man had. But Franklin knew Pete had nothing to tell. The real stories of every great fish in Pete's mind were not to be told; he possessed a silent collection of images he was unable to describe because it was too wonderful and beautiful for him to talk about. He had to keep something for himself.

Franklin understood this. And he knew his own fishing stories did not exist. He had none. They belonged to his father and the man was finished. Franklin had a son, Benjamin, who was not going to hear stories but see things as they happened.

The luck is with me now, Franklin thought, the true, honest fishing luck that one must have to connect. It was not extraordinary luck or superstition, not something few people had. It was luck in the way that luck is the willingness to give oneself over to the experience, and the willingness to do things differently than before.

He said so to Elaine that night as they went to bed. Now the luck is with me, he said.

How?

Because it's the real thing now.

She was not sure what he meant. She didn't ask because he seemed pleased enough with himself to leave it at that.

Six

The Midnight Fish

Let's go striper fishing, George said.

My friend George works at a bar, ordering booze and keeping inventory, and doesn't waste words. When three beer trucks pull up at once, he nods, says, Beer. When I show him a photograph of a big fish, he says, Nice.

So when he said, Let's go striper fishing, the use of a verb meant he was serious. He is serious about fishing. Intense, actually.

The locks to the north were closed and the boulders in the flat bend where we fished on the Saluda River appeared like half-buried giant turtles. George stopped on a big flat rock. He looked like a totem pole in his chest waders with his skinny long arms and legs. He nodded at a couple of men in the distance. They're on our spot, he said, but they'll go in a minute.

We waited. The sky glowed orange with the light from the nearby highway. A thin slice of moon shone on the water in a glittery smear. The two men finally packed up and walked past us, nodded, and disappeared, and we went down to our spot.

George used a big red-white Bomber. I took up a flashlight and ran it up and down the body of the plug I tied on to light up its inner fluorescent strip. The plug glowed like a fat lightning bug.

Down the bank were two other guys. I saw their flashlight beams. I clicked my light twice. They clicked back. About 100 yards up river I saw another dot of yellow light, and across the river as well were several flashlight dots, in there in the trees. Not everybody had left.

George hit quick and his fish ran with a loud drag buzz. The fish went with the current, weighing itself down with water and then splashing on the surface and running again. After a while George had the fish in a pool in front of us. In my flashlight beam the fish shone like some long piece of mica-layered jade. Its eyes were gold. George put it on his stringer.

Nothing happened for a while. Mosquitoes buzzed around my boonie hat. I cast and made that long first pull to get that streak of lure, water, and light that catches a striper's eye. Nothing hit. I opened a beer.

Suddenly from down-water came shouts and the sizzle of drag. In the dark below someone bellowed, Hooooo!

George perked up. He said, Midnight fish. From the distance the water amplified the rattle-smash of bottles, boots slapping stone, and someone falling and cursing.

George said, with rare pleasure, Big one. Damn, boy. Hope he's got enough line.

For about five minutes we listened to the scramble—one guy with the fish, and another man sloshing in the water, speaking in high whispers, Yeah, yeah, keep that line.

I saw the shapes of the men against the blue-black water. The rod whipped like a long reed and the fish breached—a flash of white out there in the open, moonlit river.

Everyone on the river watched. I saw flashlights blinking on, the beams zipping around as people searched tackle boxes, changing lures, trying to guess what the big fish had hit.

I put my rod up on a rock and went down to the men fighting the fish. One guy was in the shallows. In the beam of my light I saw his face; he was tall, big, and looked like Larry Holmes, the prize fighter. I shot the beam at the other man, his sunburned neck shining.

What's he got? I said.

The big guy said, The biggest striper ever caught. Then he turned to his friend and said, Come on, Daryl, come on, man.

Daryl, up to his armpits in the river, shouted, I'm floating.

The big guy and I dashed into the shallows and began pulling the rotund, buoyant Daryl by his shirt as the striper pulled in the opposite direction. We stood Daryl on his feet and he sat on a small boulder. The fight was really on, the heavy monofilament playing sharp notes against the guides of the bowed rod, the drag buzzing then stopping, then buzzing again. Daryl and the big guy, Chuck, shivered. I shivered too.

For a tense half hour that huge fish dove and pulled, ran and circled with the seeming force of a killer whale. The three of us sitting on the rocks began to wonder if this was going to ever end, and if we should give up and cut the line. But we knew everyone on the river was watching us; this had become an event with a small, exclusive audience waiting in the darkness. Chuck and Daryl talked high-pitched, fast, and called each other names so you'd think they hated each other. Damn you, Daryl. Up yours, Chuck.

A few other people had gathered around, very interested, George among them. One fellow—stringy yellow hair, Allman Brothers t-shirt, can of Miller—he offered to go back to his truck and get a high-powered rifle with a scope and he'd shoot the fish when it jumped. Chuck had to hold Daryl down when he heard this suggestion and I had to take the rod as Daryl thrashed and cursed the guy while everyone else laughed. The blonde fellow slowly walked away. Daryl and Chuck wrestled in the water, then Daryl looked at me and shouted, Who the hell are you anyway?

Your long lost cousin come to help you catch this fish, I said.

The fish lunged deep in the current and I worked the rod. Daryl shouted, Give me that, and took the big fiberglass Shimano from me.

The pull on the end of that line was unnatural. It felt like some man-made thing was down there, pulling me under with industrial force. When I gave the rod back to Daryl my hands were hot.

I climbed out of the water, back onto the big rock. George said nothing. His eyes were scanning the deep plain of water spread below us like left field. The fish was out there in that water, turning slowly. The situation was hardly in hand but Daryl was doing better. He had gained line steadily in the last twenty minutes. As I looked out the striper rose to the top of the black river and thrashed up a wave of foam. Everyone on the river saw it and we all moaned and whooped as if we were at a church revival. Striper fishing can do that to you.

All along other people on the river hooted their own triumph as they lifted fish from the river. Others called out to us as a hooked fish streaked toward Daryl's monster and we all feared they would cross, double back, and it would all go to hell. But somehow, underneath there in the impenetrable black, the fish cleared one another in their struggles like kites tilting in a stiff wind.

Minutes to midnight, we were all in the water up to our waists, flashlights in hand, the fish in close. We had lit up the giant once and saw under the surface only a great swath of gold-white. It made a plunging dive and Daryl slipped and was under, and Chuck, George, and I rushed over and pulled him up and kept the rod bent. Daryl came sputtering, soaked and shiny in the bare light. He didn't talk. He breathed in long intakes through his nose and muttered to himself. The big rod whipped and nodded as the fish turned, dove down then up as if summoning from the river itself the strength for another big run.

Then the fish was in the shallows around the rocks where we stood weary and fish-mad. Daryl gave the rod to Chuck and swam out, and Chuck cried, No, Daryl, man, no—but Daryl was going face-to-face with this fish.

We lit up the water with our flashlights and watched as Daryl bent, chest-deep, and tried to round up his fish. The beast was a great dark-to-light shape in the water. It was not to be cornered; it loomed and turned and Daryl was too short and too buoyant to do anything. He came back and we watched the fish appear on the surface, so big, so close to us. Daryl looked again and saw the fish. He lunged and performed the unheard of: he got with the fish—he flung himself and hugged himself to it and squealed when the spikes stabbed him in the chest. He rushed it into a shallow pool, bellowing, Oh, god, oh, lord, oh, god.

George snorted with both dislike and amazement. We all splashed into the pool, flashlight beams whipping.

Daryl was atop a striper that was more pig-like than fish-like. Its tail flapped and it bulged its head out of the water. We grabbed Daryl and hauled him along with the fish. He pulled it out and laid it on a flat rock.

We stood around the striper in silence. Even the

silence that came from George was a stunned silence. The few people behind us gasped. It was like a scene from a Winslow Homer painting: men in some semi-wilderness, standing around a great, big fish, our faces dumb but our eyes like little fires, the fish's body a long flag of black and white, green, and gold. A big silver Rapala stuck out its mouth like a fatal cigar.

Chuck and Daryl stopped panting and looked at each other then began whooping and clapping. Other people called out to us and shouts about the size of the fish echoed up and down the river: How big? Fifty pounds! How big? Five feet! Who got it? I got it, Daryl cried. I got it. Me!

In the combined light of our flashlights Daryl bent to unhook the striper and we saw exactly how big the fish was. It seemed as large as a side of beef. Its colors were distinctive, the white of its belly meeting in an exact line the olive of its flanks, and its lateral black stripes that flashed gold between were as long as a man's belt. Its eyes were gold. It appeared powerful enough to have dragged all of us to the bottom.

We jumped around and slapped each other on the back and called out. But we were forgetting to kill this fish, and a fish this big you've got to kill like a bear—shoot twice.

As Daryl danced he realized the fish was dancing too, up on its tail, throwing itself toward the river. Our victory shouts became screams of outrage as we charged into the splash the fish made. We rolled and slapped in the shallows, tearing ourselves on the rocks and getting speared by fish spines. We grabbed and grabbed, George like a crazed parrot chattering, Taxidermist, taxidermist.

Daryl grabbed the fish and jammed his hands into its gills. The rest of us grabbed on. We dragged the fish back onto the rocks. Glazed with a kind of madness, Daryl picked up a rock and with a Cro Magnan stroke smashed the fish twice between the eyes. The fish shook, shuddered, crapped all over Daryl, then flopped over in his arms.

We were victorious. And wet. A little cold. A little drunk. Bloody. Crapped on. And victorious.

George calmed for a moment then began to shudder and he chattered over his clicking teeth, Got...to get...taxidermist's.

He and I ran and grabbed our gear, then grabbed their gear as Chuck and Daryl prepared to haul the fish up the bank. They took a thick branch from a fallen limb and stuck it through the fish's gills and out its mouth. George said, Ice, ice.

I thought George was going to have a heart attack. He was young but talking too much.

All four of us trundled up the steep bank to where we had parked our cars. George and I lead the way, arms full of gear, rods slapping the tree branches. Near the top came a sharp crack from behind and Chuck shouted, Oh, *no*.

I looked back to see the broken stick and the fish sledding down the mud and over the the rocks back to the river. With a wail of horror we threw ourselves down the bank.

The fish slipped into a shallow pool and bobbed there like a sinking ship. Just as we came atop it, the fish shuddered once then kicked with its tail and it sent itself between two rocks into a deeper pool. We jammed and jumbled over the rocks like madmen, screaming in fright that the fish was going to get away. The fish began to propel itself, belly-up as it was, toward the water that flowed into the current. We splashed and kicked and leapt on top of that big fish.

Sloppily, heaving, we got the fish to the rocky bank again. Daryl took a stringer and tied the fish through the mouth and around the gill, then bound the other end to his wrist; he was going with this fish wherever it went even if it sank or burst into flame. Daryl and Chuck went slowly over the rocks and up the bank as if carrying their sick mother to the car. George and I climbed to his car, the big blue LTD, and put our gear and our friend's gear in the backseat. Then Chuck and Daryl got into an argument where they stood at the back of Chuck's old 280Z.

Chuck said, Like hell I'm putting that fish in there. It's gonna get in the carpet and stink. Tie it to the roof.

That's no good, Daryl squealed.

George stepped in—Get some tree branches. Line the thing with branches.

We snapped to action like the Three Stooges and filled Chuck's hatchback with leafy sweetgum branches. Chuck and Daryl lifted the magnificent fish into the hatch and it weighed down the back of the car.

Got to get ice, George said.

Where? Daryl said.

Green's, George said. Bags of ice.

Soon we were speeding back into Columbia.

Green's is a massive liquor and beer store set strategically between downtown and the football stadium. One side of the store is all liquor, the other side beer and wine, and on the beer side is the ice cooler.

We spun into the parking lot and jumped out. The face of a young woman minding the register grew wide with astonishment as she watched four men grab madly for every bag of ice they could carry. She became doubly astonished when Daryl went over to her to ask if she would sell him one of the big grey plastic barrels they sat beer kegs in.

As the woman explained that such barrels came as part of the rental of a keg, George suddenly exclaimed—Look.

The 280Z was bouncing. We saw the large black shape inside thrashing in a salad of elm branches. The striper was lashing blood and slime and fish crap all over the dashboard, tape deck, and bead-covered seats of Chuck's bachelor machine. No number of *Penthouse* magazine air fresheners could ever cut the odor that was to remain.

Chuck dropped the ice and ran out the door. George, Daryl, and I followed with what ice we had. Chuck and Daryl jammed themselves through the doors, George and I through the hatch, and we began beating the fish with the ice bags as Chuck grabbed it by the head. The fish was not to be stilled and it swung side-to-side then with an incredible arching snap flung itself upward into the ceiling and slapped itself across our faces. Our curses and blows rained down until a woman's screaming behind us caught our attention. We looked back.

Outside the beer store stood the clerk. She was screaming with her hands smacked against the side of her face. Then she pointed at us and yelled, They're killing him! Those men are killing a freak in that car!

We looked at ourselves as if to ask, Are we really? We almost believed her. We looked back at the store, our faces confused and shining with slime, and we saw a big, bearded white guy, the owner, come out to look at what his clerk screamed about. When he saw three guilty-looking crackers and one guilty-looking black man standing around an old 280Z surrounded by scattered ice-cubes he assumed the worst. He grabbed the woman, jumped back inside, and locked the door.

We didn't stay to see if the fellow actually dialed 911: his very expression cried, *Police*. We jumped in our cars and gunned out of the parking lot.

George was getting very overwrought—I knew because he repeated himself, saying, Got to get it in ice. Color's gonna fade. I began to worry if his usually near-dead resting pulse could handle the strain. The old LTD almost didn't. It was burning oil and taking the turns on its worn tires as well as a sofa on wheels. When George accelerated to keep up with the speeding 280Z, the old four-barrel didn't so much thunder as groan.

We saw Chuck and Daryl whip into the parking lot of the Food Lion on Harden Street, the bottom of the car lighting up with sparks as they went over a speed bump. We parked side-by-side and got out. Daryl said, I'll stay with the fish. You guys go get the ice.

As we gathered bags of ice and beer, we were followed by nasty stares and wrinkled faces from the nice evening food shoppers. In the check-out line, a little boy riding in a cart looked up at me, pinched his nose and said, Peee-U.

The check-out clerk said, You guys been fishing, huh?

Chuck said loudly, We just caught the biggest striper in all of South Carolina.

Smells like you been sleeping with the biggest you-know-what in all of Carolina.

Chuck shoved the cash into the young man's chest and we walked away. As we went out the sliding doors, we nearly dropped everything in shock because there were two police officers talking to Daryl, their cruiser blocking our cars. The flickering blue lights lit up the parking lot. Chuck started to mumble. We walked up to the two cops and to Daryl, who was starting to sweat. One of the cops said to Chuck, This your car?

Yessir, it's mine.

The other officer said, We got a report that there was some sort of assault going on in this car. This fellow here—the officer nodded at Daryl—says you were just killing the fish in there. That right?

Yessir, Chuck said. The fish wasn't dead. We were just throwing ice on it, that's all.

We all began to relax because the cops seemed to relax, a tiny bit anyway.

Chuck continued, Yeah, you bet. Daryl here caught this fish and we think it's a record. Got to be. Weighs over forty...pounds, Chuck said, pausing to look at Daryl who was making faces and pointing with a tiny finger motion at Chuck, then at himself, shaking his head, then pointing back at Chuck.

The taller, blonder cop said to Chuck, This guy says you caught the fish.

Chuck, George, and I looked at Daryl: Daryl forced a smile, his brow, face, and neck glistening with sweat in the orange lamp light. He said, I...I was trying to take credit, officers, you know? But really, he caught it. I just helped.

It dawned on us that Daryl did not have a fishing license.

The cops turned to Chuck. So you caught it? one of them said.

Chuck put down the bags of ice, nodding, saying, Yes, yes, I did most of the fighting, yes, and Daryl, he helped with the net and dragging the fish out. I was just trying to make him feel good by saying that he, you know—I was just kidding him cause he coulda caught one this big but I caught this one and—

Who are you guys? the cop said to me and George.

Just friends, I said.

Needed ice, George said. To stuff it.

The cops exchanged quick cop glances, not really looking at each other but looking at each other just the same. The big one shrugged, looked in the car at the dead fish, and said, Well, they said at the liquor store that you guys were assaulting someone.

We were trying to put ice on the fish, Daryl said.

In the car? the shorter, younger cop said.

Gotta stuff it, George said.

The cop nodded. Another cruiser pulled up and two more cops got out, walked over and exchanged cop glances with the cops already with us. The big blonde cop said to Chuck, All right. Just show me your fishing license and ev'ything'll be fine.

I knew, of course, that Chuck too did not have a fishing license. I let out a long sigh that George understood. I knew he wanted to jump in and say that he was the one who caught the fish, but then another change in the story would surely land us in jail. So George and I slowly moved to our car, sat on the hood and opened a beer each and took a long pull, and then a cop came over and confiscated the beers because the city had just passed an Open Container Law. So we sat there on the hood of the old LTD, stinky, slimy, and dry, watching poor Chuck root through his stinky, slimy car in desperate hopes that he would find a fishing license left there by the previous owner of the 280Z and maybe the cops would let us go, even though cops really have nothing to do with fish and game laws. Two more cops showed up, and then a photographer from the newspaper. George began to sputter, the blue police lights flashing across his face.

The next morning I got up and showered again. Then I stood in the living room in my shorts trying to sniff my face, and sniffing my arms and hands. I wasn't sure if I still reeked or not because by then fish smell molecules were in my brain and I was like a gas station attendant who can't smell gas by the end of the day. I leaned out the screen door to pick the newspaper off the porch. The paper, flung by a weak paperboy, was on the steps and I scampered down, grabbed it, someone honked at me from the street, and I went back inside and sat down.

There it was on the front page: a photograph of six cops and the Midnight Fish, the cops' smiles wide, the fish faded in death, its oily gleam seared away by the flashbulb so it looked like a long piece of tattered, greasy cloth.

I remembered Daryl's anguished groans and curses as Chuck combed the bottom of his car, the glove compartment, and his pockets for some piece of paper that had something to do with fishing. Daryl started to cry when the photographer told the cops to pose with the fish. They held it up on the end of a billy club.

The article headline read:

Columbia Cops Confiscate Record Striper

The story ran:

> Four Columbia police officers caught this record striper last night and they weren't even fishing. They took the fish from a man who didn't have a license.
> The man, Chuck Lawton, 37, of Lexington, caught the fish illegally in the Saluda River and was trying to find ice to preserve the fish for mounting when the officers discovered what he had in the back of his car while parked at the Food Lion on Harden St. after Lawton and three

friends had gone to Green's Liquor Emporium trying to get ice there.

Lawton was charged with taking fish without a license and was fined by Fish and Game officers who were contacted by the police.

Lt. D.D. Colby said the fish weighed 60 pounds 9 ounces when he put it on a scale in the police department mail room. "That's a new state record," he said, "if it were legal. But since [Lawton] didn't catch the fish legally, the fish don't exist."

The big fish was confiscated by Fish and Game.

Two other men, Len Stanton, 26, and George Oswald, 32, both of Columbia, were charged with possession of open containers of alcohol and arrested at the scene. They each pled no contest in night court and paid each a $100 fine.

All three men and a fourth man, Daryl Long, were charged with petty theft but the charges were dropped when the four paid for the ice they had taken from Green's Liquor Emporium.

I let out an agonized sigh. I decided not to call my girlfriend. I took greater pleasure in thinking about her finding out the news from her friends who were surely calling her that very minute, telling her she was truly dating a bum, rather than going and telling her that myself. Instead I called George.

Did you see the paper? I said.

He stuttered, then asked, Going tonight?

You cleaned out? I said.

My last hunnert, he said.

Okay, I'll get the beer.

SEVEN

Sunnies

They didn't have a name yet. But they wanted to have a name for the infant the minute they saw their child's face.

They were sitting by the pond beneath the hill. It was hot for June. The baby was due on July fourth, two weeks away.

Jean did not think she was able to endure the rest of the month. Her body sometimes felt like a bulky, steamy greenhouse that she occupied along with the thumping, rolling being inside. They could reach and touch each other but were both invisible in the humid gloom.

Jean lay on a blanket in the shade of a tulip tree near the water. She had on a floppy straw hat and a sun dress that she liked and didn't like. She liked its pattern and design yet was bothered that it seemed to her like a mu-mu draped over a car. She didn't want to be pregnant anymore. She wanted a baby.

Her man, Hank, was sitting on the grass with his feet hanging over the edge of the bank, his toes dipped in the water, tempting the snapping turtles. He was fishing, stripped down to his cut-off blue jeans, his frizzy blonde hair pulled back in a tight pony tail. He sat sideways to Jean. She watched his lean muscles contract and relax, a sheen of sweat across his freckled skin. She looked back and forth from him to the big bucket he had behind him, pressed into the soft soil.

The fish in the bucket were small opal tiles. The bucket was clear plastic, tall and wide, and when it was full of clear pond water it was very heavy. Hank had nearly fallen in the pond scooping water. But he had strong arms and hands. He was a carpenter who had a job with a house-builder. He had brought the bucket back from his last job. A scientist was remodeling his house and threw out some old equipment. Hank said he took the big bucket for just this purpose: to keep sunnies for the afternoon.

Hank was using a #10 hook to catch small ones and put them in the bucket when he caught them. Sometimes he pulled in a stout bluegill and he threw it back. But when he brought up a little pumpkinseed, he put it in the bucket and put back the flat lid with holes punched in it.

Jean watched the little fish slowly turn. One of them was swimming mad corkscrews along the edge of the bucket from top to bottom. It stopped, gulped, bumped another fish then began again, diving and coming back up, round and round. Jean said, Hank, there's a spastic fish in there.

Hank looked over. He saw the fish swimming wildly. He set down his rod, took off the bucket lid, and reached in. Gingerly he captured the fish in his cupped hand and pulled it up along the bucket side, then held him in the sun. He said, Go back, spaz, and slipped the fish into the pond.

The pond sat in the shadow of the hill at Hank's back. Across the pond from where he sat was a tall stand of trees, the beginning of a large, rolling woods that covered the hills. Far above the trees a glossy black vulture wheeled against the clouds. The day was sunny and quiet except for the sounds of occasional stone trucks rumbling down the river road a distance away. Brown grasshoppers made flicking noises in the grass.

Hank looked back to his bobber. He was using a short, whippy rod and tiniest open-face reel he was able to find at the sport shop in Hopewell where he lived. The silver reel was about as big as the inner mechanism of a kitchen coffee grinder.

The bobber on the water was a little bubble, yellow on the top, orange on the bottom, the black spring plunger in the middle. It looked like some sort of berry. When the sunnies nibbled the bobber did a little dance. Hank had caught salmon in Alaska, and stripers in the river, but for him nothing was more keen than watching the tiny, black-eyed bobber nod, toddle, slide off and slip under.

He watched as the bobber nodded and moved straight away from the bank. He had the bail open and waited until the bobber went down to turn the handle, flick the rod and set the hook. He grunted when he saw it was a big one. He played it. He liked that sunnies never surfaced or jumped. Just pure fight, the fish not to be taken from the water until totally overpowered, formidable no matter how small.

Hank pulled the fat, dark bluegill out of the water. It fit flat in his palm. He unhooked it and tossed it back. He looked at the little Kirby hook. Only a bit of worm remained. He opened the big yogurt container and probed with his fingers to find another worm.

Jean put her hand on the mound of her belly. The baby had been unusually quiet. It moved when Jean moved but otherwise rested. She imagined she would spend another night serving as the little thing's trampoline. Jean said, How about Jessica? If it's a girl?

Hank focused on getting half a worm to break off,

sliding the hook into the slimy thing. He said, I don't like it.

Why?

I already told you.

I forgot, she said.

Because in the ninth grade a girl named Jessica said she liked me then went to the movies with someone else, so I don't like the name. It sounds sinister.

It's not sinister.

Yes it is.

Jean repositioned herself. Possibly the most irritating part part of pregnancy was that a given posture or lounging of body became tiring much sooner than it should. She needed, she decided, a juggernaut. Yes, a prenatal juggernaut equipped with a fat vinyl chair filled with gel she could sit on and ooze into, suspended like the baby inside her. Several young men built like Arnold Schwartzenegger would bear this juggernaut wherever she told them to go. She had managed to finish teaching the school year, and she imagined herself arriving at Bear Tavern Elementary School atop a juggernaut born by six Conan barbarians every spring morning. The students would have come out and cheered.

She stared into the glassy bucket of sunnies. They were such lovely fish. Truly lovely, she thought, much more pleasing than any tropical fish she had seen. Her father had kept three tanks of tropical fish and she thought them useless. They were all either black, black and silver, white, or purple, and they died in droves.

The sunnies were vital. If they survived year after year in a small pond at the foot of a big, rocky hill in the middle of nowhere near the Delaware river, they surely would survive in a pristine, well-filtered tank. Their bodies were narrow but strong. The wild fish were beaded and flashing, their colors true colors, Jean realized. If she wanted to teach her students or teach her unborn child what orange was, she would show them a bit of the breast of a sunny. And if she wanted to teach them turquoise, she would show them its face and cheek.

She said to Hank, Jeannie? How about Jeannie?

I like that better. Yeah, that's good. Have you said that before?

No, I don't think so. I'd remember if you had liked it.

How about just Jean?

That's my name, Jean said.

Sure. Why not?

It's kind of weird. Daughters aren't ever named after mothers.

I like your name, Hank said.

What about Deborah?

Too sexy.

Sexy? Jean said, turning to rest on her other side as she watched Hank drop another pumpkinseed, a tiny, coin-sized fish, into the clear bucket. She said, Deborah is not a sexy name. It's just a nice name.

Deborah is sexy. It sounds like heavy breaths, he said, flipping the hook back into the pond.

What's wrong with our daughter having a sexy name?

Hank did not think of a good reason. After all, a daughter would one day grow into a woman. He shook his head, getting ahead of himself and the unborn baby. He still didn't like Deborah. He said, Let's talk about boys' names.

Do you like Hank for a boy's name?

Mmmm, he murmured. He was watching the bobber nod and slide to the left. He snapped the rod and held the fish in check as it turned again and again. He fished

this one out easily. It was very small and foul-hooked in
the side of the mouth. He held the little sunny between
his fingers and thumb and wondered if someone could
fire glazed terra-cotta slabs in the pattern of the beautiful little fish. Laying perfect tile was Hank's particular
specialty beyond carpentry. He imagined an entire floor
and wall space tiled with little tiles of perfectly glazed
ceramic in the colors of pumpkinseeds.

Jean lifted herself from reclining on her side to sitting with her knees wide. She had decided to give birth
on her hands and knees. The midwives at the birthing
center she and Hank attended recommended this posture over laying on her back to deliver. She wasn't sure
if she liked such a position, though, because she would
give birth like a cow. But she had been told that it was a
good position for a lot of women, that way or squatting.

A breeze blew up her dress and was very nice over
her humid skin. She gazed at the swimming sunnies.
She wondered if they could take some home and put
them in an aquarium. She said, Would you like to get an
aquarium? We could put sunnies in it.

Hank nodded and smiled over his shoulder. I was just
thinking about that, he said. I'll have to see if anyone
has an old aquarium and filter system laying around.
Lots of people do, in their attics or cellars. I could find a
really big old tank and a pump and filter and get them
running again. Of course, it's illegal to keep wild fish
like that.

No it isn't, Jean said.

Sure it is. It's a law, he said.

Jean inched forward on her buttocks, keeping her
belly from rocking her over. She wrapped her legs
around Hank from behind and put her arms around his
chest. She put her face against his back, his perspiration
sealing her cheek to him. She said, If it's a girl, we'll

name her Sunny. How about that?

He laughed and she felt his muscles tighten when he laughed. I'm serious, she said.

Sounds like a hippy name.

We're hippies.

Us? We have jobs. You're a school teacher. You've got tenure.

You've got a pony tail.

I like my hair long.

Is Sunny better than Deborah? Jean said, mouthing the words against his shoulder blade.

Yes. I'll admit it is. But what would the kid think when she finds out she's named after a fish?

They're nice fish. Sunny for a girl, Hank for a boy.

Do you want to name him Henry and call him Hank, like me?

Hank's a cute name for a little boy.

The problem is, it sticks, Hank said. No one would ever call me Henry now, no one except grandpop.

They were quiet for a long time, Jean resting her face against his back, adjusting her breathing and their baby's breathing to his so all three breathed together. Hank's breathing quickened when the bobber disappeared.

The bobber had shot away and sank and something was trying to run, not turn like a sunfish. Hank reeled against the fish and it wheeled around in the thick algae and jumped out of the water, a small bass. Hank soon had it by its jaw. He unhooked it and threw it back. He put the rod down. The fishing was done. He could have gone on until the snow fell catching sunnies one after one. The bass was the signal that the day was over. Eighteen sunnies swam in the bucket.

He leaned back into Jean and she tucked her head against his, cheek to cheek. He said, If the baby is here on time, we could get married in September. That would be enough time after the birth.

I want to get married at Christmas, she said.

Why?

Because it would be nice. Christmas present to our parents.

Okay, Christmas. No one will be building houses then. I'll have more time. So will you.

Sarah, she said. Sarah for a girl, Hank for a boy.

Yeah. Sarah or Hank.

We'll never tell her we almost named her after a fish.

You really think it's going to be a girl, don't you?

Yes, Jean said.

Hank smiled. He felt her belly and breasts pressed into him, and he felt how elastic her big belly was. He liked to press himself against her womb and feel the baby push against him, but this day the baby was being still, probably napping, enjoying the air. He wondered why no one was able to remember being tucked in that tight, dark space for so long.

Jean had her legs wrapped under Hank's, her hands over his belly as she kissed his neck. The weight of their bodies together had changed the soft slope of earth by minuscule degrees, enough to set the fish bucket tipping. They were swept by a sudden wash of warm water and Jean shouted, and they sat up in constellation of bright, springing fish.

We've got to get them back in, Jean said. They'll hurt themselves. She struggled to stand, trying to balance herself without stepping on a fish. Hank was laughing and Jean said, Come on, Hank, help me, but she was laughing too.

The flashing sunnies tried to swim in the clover leaves, some snapping themselves up like hot pieces of metal buckling and snapping off a sun-scorched roof. Hank and Jean picked them up quickly and tossed them into the pond. He told her to be careful of the spines. She picked them up the way he did, gripping them carefully with her thumb and finger over the gills. Make sure there aren't any we didn't see, she said, and they checked carefully through the clover, looking over honey bees in the white flowers. They found the last one, the smallest, gulping on its side in a thick patch of the dark green leaves. Jean said, I wonder if he thinks he's dying.

He knows, Hank said.

Jean picked up the fish and Hank held her free hand as she leaned awkwardly, wobbly, and laid open her hand in the water. The fish rested there for a moment and with a slow stroke of its tail it moved away. Hank pulled Jean back up and steadied her.

They searched the grass again and were certain there were none still stranded. They had put them all back in the pond.

Jean shook herself. She breathed heavily and her body flashed hot, first her thighs and legs, then her back and neck, then head. She felt the cloth over her buttocks, feeling that the whole back of her sundress was soaked with pond water. When the breeze blew, the wet cotton was cool against her legs. She felt suddenly unsettled and thrilled.

Hank put all his equipment in his backpack and they walked on the dirt path around the pond to the car. Hank drove over the hills and along valleys until they got home to the bungalow they rented in a stand of pine trees.

When they were in bed that night Jean said, Would you say I was crazy if I said that the baby would come very soon, because of the fish falling on us today?

I wouldn't say crazy, no. Clairvoyant, maybe.

I think the baby's coming.

When?

Maybe tonight.

You think so?

Yes.

Early in the morning Jean dreamed of the sunnies jumping and flipping all around in the bed with them. She tried to grab them in her hands. She poked at the wet bedclothes. Hank murmured. Jean said, The baby's coming, and her whole body tightened.

After all the pain, the baby girl was born there in the bed.

EIGHT

Mudfish

George and I were drinking beers at the bar where he was supposed to be working. George said, Let's go catch mudfish. I asked him what they were. He said, Mudfish're kinda like gar. Both're primitive. Mudfish're shaped different. Don't have a long snout.

So what's it like? I said.

George looked at me through his round, John Lennon specs and said, Looks like a torpedo. Small fins and a big round head. Head's got armor-plated scales. Mouth like a box of nails. Got an air bladder. Can breathe out of the water for a couple of days. Can't eat 'em. Taste like mud. Probably poisonous.

The usually laconic George used so many words I wondered if he were making this up. I said, A *mudfish*?

He nodded, saying, Or "grindle." Where you're from I think they call them "bowfin."

At the mention of *bowfin* my mind flashed back to a picture in a book from childhood; amid visions of dinosaurs, dragons, and sharks I saw a long, green fish with a wide, flat head and beady eyes. I said, When should we go?

Saturday. Round noon. Takes a few hours to hike to the gut.

The next Saturday afternoon we were rumbling to the Congaree Swamp in George's blue LTD. The Congaree is a national wildlife monument controlled by the feds. It's a great place. The first time I was there I thought the bald cypress were some of the most majestic trees I had ever seen.

The day was cloudy but the breeze was good. We parked outside the gates because we planned to stay past sundown. As we walked on the sandy road and passed the ranger station I looked at the Mosquito Meter, a crude dial made from wood, the pointer manually turned to one of five categories: "Great Day," "Okay," "Buggy," "Take Cover," "Don't Inhale." The red pointer pointed at "Okay"

In the gravel parking lot were minivans, pick-ups, a hatchback with a canoe precariously balanced on the roof rack, and one battered VW minibus. The swamp is a popular place. Fraternity and sorority initiations are conducted at night out in the muddy depths. Bird watchers spend entire weekends enraptured. People hike all the way to the river, get too tired to walk back, and end up wandering in the dark.

George wore old jeans over which he wore his hip waders that made him look extra tall, a long-sleeved cotton shirt, and baseball cap over his short red hair. He wore his glasses. I had on my old hunting boots, old jeans, a faded, torn denim shirt, and a boonie hat with mosquito netting tucked in the band just in case. We carried our gear in knapsacks slung over our shoulders. We had taken apart our big spinning rods and had them in homemade PVC-pipe carriers we slung along our sides like quivers. The underbrush in the Congaree is too thick for walking with a fishing rod.

Before we went far we stopped and George looked at the map. He pointed to an oblong blob in the lower right hand corner. He said, That's it. Old Dead River Gut. Flows into Horsepen Gut then flows into the river. He looked up at the sky. Little cloudy, he said, but should be a good day.

The light changed as we moved into the swamp. The massive pines blocked the sun and many smaller trees took the remaining light. Sun penetrated clearings and inroads only. This was the time of year, mid-July, when everything was its full green; we seemed to swim through deep green water.

The plank-wood walkway ended after a short distance. We continued on the soft soil. Anoles, skinks, and salamanders flickered in the dead leaves on the forest floor. A box turtle lumbered its way in some reeds. Ahead, near a stream, a red-bellied water snake shot across the path. Farther down the trail, a black coachwhip coiled itself and opened its white mouth when I approached. I wondered what the chances were of seeing a cottonmouth. Pretty good I supposed.

George, I said, are there any really dangerous animals out here?

Mostly the cottonmouths and maybe some rattlers. I've never known anyone who got bit.

So just snakes?

Horse flies can really bite. And there's some kind of hornet, reddish ones. Bad news.

What about alligators? I said.

Probably're in here, but they ain't much worry.

What about the wild boar? I said.

George stopped and looked at me. You some kind of Nelly? he said.

Just asking.

Hogs usually hear you first and move off. If one charges just get up a tree. You can side-step them too if you're quick.

I am neither quick nor a good climber, so I asked, How many times you heard of them attacking?

A few times. Sows with young. Big boars. See, George said, feral hogs're domestic pigs that run off and mated with wild ones already out here. But they're all the same. Mean.

I nodded. I remembered seeing photographs of boars hunted by Czars. The big brown animals looked like cloven-hooved bears. I wondered what a feral hog looked like.

We tucked our chins as we glided under low branches, moving with the speed of trackers certain of the spoor. The mosquitoes weren't bad. We thanked the breeze for that. I wondered if a storm would break before we left the swamp. Getting rained on is always part of the deal, but late afternoon rain storms in South Carolina at this time of year are invariably electrical storms with great blasts of lightning—strobe-bright, horribly loud, and always right on top of you.

We paused to drink water from our canteens. Some deer ran by, spooked. We took off our hats, wiped our brows, put on more Avon Skin-So-Soft which is the best mosquito repellent known, and, hats replaced, moved on. We passed over muddy streams full of blackened logs and stumps, and strode by tall stands of bamboo.

After two hours we got to Old Dead River Gut, a crescent-shaped pond about one hundred yards long and thirty yards wide. A dark stream entered at its northern end, creating a molasses-like flow that left the gut at the other end and flowed about a half mile to the next gut then on to the Congaree River. The gut was surrounded by tall cypress and many-armed oaks.

George led around to the opposite, bowed side of the gut and here he put his gear down. The sky was a solid gray and the water had turned an opaque cola. A steady breeze came from the southwest. The Spanish moss rustled. Bitterns cried and answered each other's wild cry. An owl hooted not far off.

We heard some other noise. Across the water on the opposite bank was a group of what some folks call "granolas": two young women and two young men, college kids in tye-dies, calicoes, Birkenstocks, and cut-offs, beads in their hair and rings in their ears and nostrils. They lounged on blankets amid their backpacks. George sniffed. I sniffed. The granolas were enjoying a banquet of wine, cheese, and very fragrant reefer.

When the they noticed George and I they stopped talking and froze a moment. Then one of the young women waved. George waved back, and I did too. One of them called, Hey, and we called back. They seemed satisfied George and I weren't rangers, SLED agents, or FBI men because they went back to eating, drinking, and laughing. Every now and then one of them stole a glance at George and me then turned back.

I set up a fish-finder rig like George: a straight line down to a sinker, and a ten-inch, heavy mono leader tied to the line about a foot above the sinker. George took from a packet a long-shanked, 1/0 double hook and said, I got really good bait.

He flipped open his knapsack and took out a package wrapped in tin foil. Res'trant ordered a bunch of trout, he said. Fish defrosted during shipment. So I took them.

Inside the folded foil were over a dozen medium-sized, gutted rainbow trout, their skin, fins, and heads still intact. I was surprised that the owner of restaurant and bar, a fellow known for his cost-cutting ways, had let a load of trout go because they had possibly spoiled. The unfrozen trout smelled all right to me. I wondered if George had stolen them from the restaurant refrigerator.

George held one up. Supposed to be used for some

French poached-trout dish, he said and snickered. He shoved the long-shanked hook up the trout's vent and forward out its mouth. The two hook points curled below the tail. George poked the heavy mono leader through the hook eye and tied it with a clinch knot. I guessed a bowfin would eat a rainbow trout though any fish in this gut surely had never seen nor smelled a trout.

We cast into the water then set our rods in Y-shaped sticks stuck in the mud. We pulled together grass and strips of bark to sit on and each took a sip from the flask filled with tequila, then we waited, the baitfishing trance upon us.

I listened to the sounds of the swamp, cries and hoots of bitterns and owls mostly, and the occasional loud laughs of the young people at their picnic. The swamp seemed almost quaint. I prayed that somewhere out there, maybe, were still a good number of bobcats. I was not hopeful enough to pray that some nights a puma crept through. They were gone.

I said, George, ever heard of the Questing Beast?

Don't think so.

It's from the Legend of King Arthur. There were these goofy guys, washouts from knighthood. They chase after this animal that they can't catch. They're never supposed to catch it but they come very close again and again and never get it. That's the Questing Beast.

George sucked in on his cigarette and said, Quest is the goal, huh? Let me tell you, anybody who believes that kind'a crap is scared of his own destiny—and he shot his arm out to grab his rod but stopped. He waited. The rod tip trembled again. He picked it up and in one motion wound the bail shut and snapped the rod with his wrist and the rod bent, the line twanging in the guides.

Something out in the dark water pulled in a slow circle. I scanned the greeny-brown surface. Nothing came up yet. George's fish bowed his rod and but took no line.

Pretty good fish, I said.

Might be our'n, George said. He pulled hard on the rod and backed up the soft bank and with a final thrashing the fish arrived. It was a big catfish. We both shrugged.

George, are you sure there's mudfish out here? I said.

He nodded, looking down at the twisting black cat. He said, Catfish is a tough cuss. He can breathe out of water too, you know.

It's not a mudfish, I said. A bowfin. A million-year old fish.

George unhooked the big cat and threw it back. He adjusted the battered trout and cast it out. I checked my line. Nothing.

We sat back down on our grassy mats. I asked George if he believed in the Loch Ness monster. He said if it was there we would have already caught it.

Have you ever see anyone catch bowfin out here? I said.

George said, I used to see this black fella in a wheelchair fishing the stream back near where the old ranger station used to be. This fella would eat them. I'd never heard of anybody eating mudfish. But this fella knew what to do. He had this nurse with him—this woman had to push this old cuss in his wheelchair all the way down the access road to the stream. When he pulled one out, the nurse strung it up on a tree branch and gutted it and bled it. That's the secret. All the guts and blood give a mudfish bad bad taste. Spoils the flesh right away. Bleed them and gut them. Then you can cook them. If you know how.

Know how to cook them? I said.

Nope. Never tried. I asked the fella and he looked at me and said, You don't need to be eating no mudfish. Guess he figured I'd come catch his mudfish. People're defensive about their fishing holes.

We sat in silence. George blew cigarette smoke over the water and it collided in the breeze with the smoke coming over the water from the college kids. One of the girls was looking us. She got up, grabbed a backpack and walked around the gut through the trees. She came up to us shyly, wearing cutoffs and a calico halter top. She wore a navel ring. She said, Hey. Would you guys like some bread and grapes?

George smiled his weak, shy smile and said, That's very nice of you.

The girl plunked down on her bottom and opened her backpack. She said her name was Carrie. I brought some wine too, she said. Her accent was a very proper young Southern white woman's accent, but here she was with swamp mud splashed over her feet and up her shins. She smiled at us, her eyes wide and red. You guys aren't rangers or anything? she said.

I told her we were professional fishermen from the National Geographic Angling Institute sent to the swamp to catch million-year-old fish.

No way, she said.

I nodded, popping a grape in my mouth.

What kind of fish? she asked.

Bowfin, I said.

They can't be a million-years-old, she said.

Well, they haven't changed in a million-years. We don't know how long individual fish can live. Perhaps a century.

I caught George peering at me from under the brim of his hat as he ate a piece of the very good homemade bread. I realized that I was selling out our luck: I was, in a way, making fun of what we were doing and turning our fishing into an onus. If we didn't produce after my boasting, we'd look like chumps to a bunch of stoned college kids who've never caught a fish in their lives.

Excited by what I had told her, the girl, Carrie, waved to her friends and called them over. They slowly got to their feet and made their way through the trees. George gave me another look. He hated having spectators. The hunt for the mudfish was not meant to be a social event.

The other girl and the two boys arrived carrying their sandals, their feet mud-smeared. They smiled cautiously and introduced themselves as Ted, Phil, and Jo-Ann.

Carrie said, These guys are from National Geographic. They're trying to catch...what kind of fish? she said to me

Bowfin, I said.

The two boys nodded, looking at me and and George with easy smiles.

The other girl, Jo-Ann, said just above a whisper, Fishing is mean, and she went and sat on a mat of grass several yards away.

George looked at me again. If he didn't catch good mudfish, because I jinxed us, he was going to make me eat all those cold trout.

The granolas settled in and passed around a big bottle of red wine then stuffed bread and granola-fruit bars in their mouths. The one boy, Phil, who was plump, had Moon Pies too.

George and I ate more of their grapes and drank some wine. George declined an offered joint; though I've known him to indulge now and then, this was fishing, and I declined as well. For a while nothing happened as a green cloud formed around us on the ground and the clouds in the sky slowly darkened.

Then my rod suddenly twisted out of the twig holder and wagged on the ground. I set the hook hard, instinctively. The drag nickered as line went out. The fish turned again and again in strong circles, twice causing a big swirl on the surface. The pull of the fish was hard on my hands. It bulldogged me for several minutes, slowly taking line away until it had traveled to the middle of the gut. Out there it swirled on the surface again, a shiny green slash, the brightest thing to be seen under the dark sky.

The granola kids were all standing along the bank, looking and wowing. George wore that teeth-gritted smile, his finest expression of pleasure that he wore whenever he or I hooked into a big specimen of the game we sought.

And I was possessed by that very focused, heightened way of fighting a good fish, that mix of urgency, pleasure, and determination. It is the true paradox of fishing that the fight is the best part, yet it is the fight you must get done if you are to be credited with the catch, if credit is what you want.

I finally had the fish near and the water began to boil. George waded out a pace and bent over to see if he could grab it but the fish thrashed wildly, sending up a shower. We saw part of the beast. It appeared about as long as a baseball bat with a fat, loaf-shaped body. It was green. Its scales were heavy and seemed leathery. I backed up and beached the fish on the mud. Arriving suddenly, it looked like nothing I had ever seen. Its head was round and blunt, with a hard-looking mouth full of quartzy teeth. Its eyes were small and high on the sides of its head. The pectoral and pelvic fins where lobe-like, and its tail was a thick, flat paddle.

One of the boys, Phil, said, Oh, my god, it's, it's one of those, those...

Coelacanths, the other said. I read about them in Bio class.

As he looked at me George's jaw muscles tightened and pulsed. I wasn't sure if he was going to laugh or cuss. He said, Ain't no coelacanth in South Carolina. That's a mudfish.

The granolas sighed and whispered in amazement as they gathered closer. I had a wet rag under the fish's belly so I could steady it and unhook it. The fish wanted none of this and flailed its tail and body in a twisting motion that was violent and effective. I stepped back, my left hand holding the leader taut. I pulled its head up and stood over it again, grabbing its belly with the rag as George grabbed its tail.

You're hurting it, the other granola girl shouted from where she sat.

We all looked back. Her intense, unhappy face was something of an indictment. George snorted.

We turned the fish on its side in the watery mud and as I grasped it with the rag I worked the hook with the pliers. The big double hook was embedded in the corner of its mouth, the torn trout hanging off like wet paper. The mudfish twisted its head and snapped its jaws. I finally plucked one, then both hooks with a grisly pop of flesh. Free of the hook the mudfish threw a fit and when it hissed we all jumped back.

The mudfish, all ten million years of survival behind it, looked at us as if it saw through us. It huffed again, kicking its air bladder into action, its toothy mouth open. As beasts go, this one, were it much bigger, would fall between shark and alligator.

George was finally smiling his genuine happy smile. Damn nice, George said, nodding at the fish. Gonna eat it?

I grinned.

Fought, didn't it?

Yes, it did, I said, very pleased. I wanted to catch another. I stepped toward the fish and it puffed itself. I gripped it with the rag and turned its body so it faced the water. Its dark skin gleamed in the pale light that came through the clouds, and its flanks flashed a green-gold color as it rolled its body. I pointed it into the shallows. It meandered into the dark water and was gone.

The granolas were impressed. But from behind us, Jo-Ann said, It's mean what you're doing. You're hurting them.

I didn't say anything. George didn't even look at her. We kept fishing. We ate some bread and grapes. We thanked Carrie who smiled at us with bleary eyes.

Then George hooked into one. It turned back and forth in one place, pulling and pulling. Line twanged in the guides, and the dimple of water where the line cut the surface trembled, moving this way and that. These were fine, powerful fish. They may not have fought as magnificently as stripers, but they made up for it in sheer aggressive resistance.

After some hard pulling on his rod and reeling line in short bursts, George had the fish close but not on the surface. I had waited to bait my hook in case George needed help, but now he appeared to nearly have the fish in hand so I went ahead and began to hook up another trout.

I looked up at the sky, worrying about an electrical storm. Maybe if I hadn't been looking up I would have been able to grab the girl.

I saw the small knife in her hand just the way Oswald's lawyer must have seen Jack Ruby's gun. I heard the distinct twang of a taut line severed and heard George shout. And somehow the girl, Jo-Ann, grabbed the rod out of his hands and ran off with it. She sprinted

into the trees and kept going, George standing there
looking at his empty hands then to the water where his
mudfish had been boiling seconds before.

The other kids were stunned, intoxicated amazement
spreading over their faces. George looked like he had
been slapped. I don't know how I myself appeared. I
thought I might laugh.

George began jumping and shouting. He jumped
and shouted in place like a preacher caught in the spirit.
Then he and I, followed by the granolas, broke through
the green leaves and started running in the darkness of
the swamp forest.

We quickly caught up with Jo-Ann. She had run a
good pace and stopped in the middle of a cathedral of
cypress, a high slope of ground in front of her. She saw
us coming and she turned and hurled the big Fenwick
like a javelin into the dense brush. When she turned
back to face George, she howled at him with a gurgling
voice not unlike a panther and ran further up the slope.
Then she shouted, Stop!

We stopped.

The young woman, who I guessed was possibly halfway through college and had enough education to be
dangerous, began her rant by saying, I have thrown
away that weapon and you cannot retrieve it. It is no
longer yours.

George let out a incredulous hiccoughy laugh. I said
nothing. Her friends tried to talk Jo-Ann down from
her perch but she shouted at them, arms out. She began
a mad speech about animal rights that went on for a
long minute and included the expressions "loving coex-
istence," and "cycle of violence."

When she was done she took a deep breath, came
down the slope of wet leaves and walked past us. She
wandered through the dense brush back to the gut.

Whatever world she was in, she was there.

George was too insulted to move; he was caught between the desire to rush at the girl and shout her to pieces, the need to find his rod, and the determination taught him by his parents not to act belligerent toward people who don't know any better. He turned in fractions of a footstep, up the slope, back to the girl, and around again, an angry Southerner.

I stepped up the slope and looked around. I saw the big black rod where it lay next to an old oak stump. A bright silver wave came through the trees and the leaves turned lavender, and a distant snap turned to a rumbling that rolled away. I muttered a curse word.

I picked up the rod and looked across the small clearing. My eyes were still filled with lavendar motes of lightning. I blinked and I still saw a large blob of hovering color that changed to a brown with black and yellow. Brown with razor hair and four yellow-black tusks.

I flew down the slope past George as he said, That storm ain't—and I heard him suck wind because he heard the pig coming with its grumbling *greee-greee-greee*. He caught up with me on those long legs and shouted to the kids ahead of us, Pig! Pig!

When the granolas turned and saw the professionals from the National Geographic Angling Institute running with definite fear on their faces, dope paranoia set in and they wailed like children and scattered in all directions—Phil and Carrie wheeling to the right—Ted turning left—righteous Jo-Ann running straight for the gut—George and I passing Jo-Ann, the rod in my hands whipping branches as we went. We filled the woods with our frightened cries and shouts, slipping, falling, turning direction and going back the way we came, trying to find the best way through the trees.

Whether the pig actually chased us or not is not a

question to be asked. In fact, I never saw the animal clearly, and in my memory it has since changed size and shape many times. But the danger of the chasing pig let loose my fear of the storm.

When the lightning fired at the river and the thunder came right behind, heavy and roaring this time, I was in for a my own bad trip. I can't explain my fear of lightning; I can't tell you how it came about or when, but I have it, irrational and over-powering.

We can hide under some trees, George said.

No way, I said.

We can hide in the stream bed.

Death trap, I said, as I took my reel out of its seat, put the rod in pieces in its case, put the reel in my knapsack, and began to buckle every pocket.

It won't last long, George said.

Right, I said, oblivious.

We can't get out of the park, Len.

I'm looking for better cover, I said.

George broke down his rod and packed his knapsack. We skirted the edge of the gut until we came to the place where we had arrived and we ran back up the trail full tilt. The storm was rushing toward us.

Lightning began to thrash down along the river far behind. The wind came swooping with a howl through the tall trees all around us as if the swamp were erupting with ghosts of dead fools killed by feral hogs. The rushing air came down around our heads and bodies like many wicked, weightless hands. The odor of the swamp, of dark soil and rotted wood, was whipped up around us. Spanish moss, leaves, and bark flew in the air and fell on us. The whole Earth seemed to be rocking off kilter. A shot of lightning exploded maybe a half mile behind, the blast like a gong hit with a sledge.

When the rain caught up with us we knew we were

in thick, solid trouble. The rain hit like pins first, then like darts, then came down like spears. The lightning was flying and sizzling behind this advance rain cloud and I did not want to look back.

I swore the lightning was going to get us because we were not going to out-run the storm. Then, ahead of us was one of the wood-plank bridges that spanned one of the many streams. This one was new, thickly built, and wide. There! I shouted.

George and I tucked ourselves tightly against the jointure of bridge and earth, knees pulled up to our chins. Here we gutted it out. Lightning slashed over and beside us in a godly blaze, down from the sky, and up out of the ground in short spikes to reach the greater arc dropping from the sky. The rain sounded like fire on the planks above our heads. So much water washed down around us the soil turned to muck and twice both of us slid down, washed into the creek, and came clawing back. We dug with our hands until we were in there like woodchucks. Thunder split our ears. The air turned to rain.

Then it was over. The lightning and thunder subsided, except for an occasional, distant roar. Everything was soaked. We were covered in mud, thick, fetid, brown swamp mud.

We climbed on top of the bridge. George brought out the flask and each of us had a few sips. As happens after these Carolina squalls, the sun came out, bright as morning.

We took off our hats, shirts, and boots and tried to clean ourselves as best we could. George took off his mud-spattered specs and began cleaning them with a bandanna.

I wonder if those kids are all right, I said.

Lord takes care of stoners, George said, with unusual charity.

We got one fish, anyway.

Mudfish're damn good, aren't they?

I nodded, my throat hot with the tequila.

Sorry I took you out in this, he said.

Sorry about that stuff about National Geographic.

George snorted.

You think that girl was right? That we torture animals?

We give these fish a contest they were born looking for, George said.

You stole those trout from the restaurant, didn't you? I said.

He nodded, smiling. Worked, didn't it?

I nodded, happy the rain and lightning were over for the day. To do right by George we hiked back to the gut so he could catch a mudfish. He did, a very big one that fought beautifully.

NINE

The Royal Coachmen

1.

Walking along a path beside the canal, seven o'clock on an April morning. Fifteen years old, with my two old Mitchell outfits, field jacket, high boots. Someone comes up behind me. When he is at my side I look over, nod, say, Good morning.

The fellow nods. He is middle-aged, pale skinned, wearing aviator eyeglasses. I take in his brown chest waders, nice vest, and the rod in his right hand. I say, What make of rod is that?

He looks at me, says, It's a fly rod.

Sure, but who makes it?

Fellow looks down at his rod. Orvis, he says.

I glance at the dark gray metallic reel. Orvis too. Bright yellow line. A Clouser's Minnow hooked in the keeper. I say, Did you tie that?

He takes the streamer in hand, and with his best text-book voice tells me, This is a Clouser's Minnow. A Susquehanna smallmouth streamer. I think the shad'll take it.

He must have bought it. Shad on that? Maybe. I wonder if I ask him the history of the fly if he would know it, and, if he does, how long-winded he'll be. I don't ask.

He says, What are you fishing for?

Trout.

In the canal? he says.

They're there, I tell him.

They ought to be. Fish and Game put 'em there, he says, looks at my rods and sees the Mepps spinners. At least you're not using worms, he says.

I ask him if he fishes for the shad every year. He says he lives in Belle Meade and was told about the shad run by some friends and that he should go fish the wing dam south of Lambertville. We move down the path and when we reach the point over the wing dam the fellow looks down the long, steep bank to the rocky outcropping where the shore meets the cement. He starts down slowly.

I consider mentioning to him that there is an easier, zig-zag trail in the trees to the right. While waiting on myself, the man tumbles from view. I look over. He manages not to break his rod on the way down. I look down the length of the dam and see several men out there with spinning outfits casting for shad and walleye. The wind whips the collars of their jackets. I wonder how many of them the fly fisher will hook in the ear and what curses they'll use.

I catch eight trout and keep four.

2.

I have a stout rainbow trout in my hands. He gobbled the spinner and I have to be a bit rough with the pliers. I get him unhooked and he flails with his tail. When I look up the yellowed grass of the canal bank I see boots. I continue looking up to see a tall, plump, pasty fellow in sparkling fly gear, holding what has got to be the longest fly rod I have ever seen. The thing must be fifteen, seventeen feet long. What the hell is he going to do with that?

Nice one, the fellow says. I thank him and dip the fish back in the water. The trout shakes his head a few times then darts off. I turn back. The man says, Have you heard of there being any bass in the river?

I look at the fly rod again. Bass? How damn big does he think the bass get around here?

He says, I heard they're catching them around Trenton.

Christ on a bike, he means the *stripers*. Big striped bass this far up river this soon? No.

I squint up at the overcast sky, the sun coming through in gaps. I say, The herring aren't here yet, but I supposed the stripers might follow the shad too. What sort of rod is that?

It's a fly rod, he says.

I know, I say. But it's got that fighting butt. Is it a striper rod?

Oh, no, no, he says. This is a two-handed casting rod. It's designed to pick up a lot of line off the water, up to eighty feet. You use both hands. I'm going fishing for salmon in the fall and I thought I'd come up here and get in some practice with the bass.

This is most presumptuous thing in my seventeen years I've ever heard anyone say with a fishing rod in his hands. You might lie about how many you caught, or how big, but I'd never heard anyone declare he wanted to *get in some practice with the bass* as if the stripers were to come jumping out in their little white shorts and knit sweaters to knock a ball around.

I look over this fellow. The hat, the polarized glasses hanging around his neck, the Nautica windbreaker, the Thinsulated fishing vest, the waders, and the boots—all of it newly minted, all of it worn exactly, all the way down to the shiny silver forceps clipped neatly to a pocket flap on his vest.

The real thing, however, is that rod, a stiff, fat blue-brown coachwhip. And that *reel*, a white drum sandwiched with line. The outfit looks so grand I think this fellow should be able to divine fish with it by pointing it at the water and following whatever way it wriggled.

I say innocently, You make two-handed casts with it?

Yes, the fellow says, enthused to tell me. You don't make false casts with this. You just pick up the line, sort of swing it to the side and get it carrying and send it back out. With both hands. That's what the extension is for. Are the bass up here yet?

No. What kind of streamers are you going to use?

The fellow unzips his vest that, I assume, must also have a built-in Mae West which inflates with the jerk of a cord. I step up the bank to stand next to him. He is unshaven and has salt-and-pepper whiskers a few days old. He wears no rings on his fingers, but has a Swiss-made outdoor wristwatch.

He unzips a little pouch like an eyeglass case and shows me multiple streamers. He picks up one in his hand, the pristine streamer encased in a clear plastic sheath. He says, This is one of the ones I had made. I've got a guy over in Langhorne who ties them.

I see through the plastic a paper card with a maker's name and Langhorne, PA, address.

The man says, This one's called the Delaware Blue-backed Herring, and he holds the streamer flat in the dull sunlight.

I look at the long fly. It has a head with a big black

eye, a skirt of blue bucktail atop, white below, and a white tube body with silver tinsel ribbing. It is very nice, tasty-looking like a candy stick. I look at some of the other streamers in the pouch and see that some are silver and red, others white, all more or less the same size, maybe four inches long. The man tells me he tied some of them himself. I nod, saying, Good show. The fellow glances at me and puts the streamer back then abruptly zips the case. I suspect you are not supposed to compliment a fly fisher.

Carelessly I say, I suppose some of the stripers could have come up this far, but I'd bet you'd sooner attract a muskie with those streamers.

You think? he says, neither pleased nor displeased.

Sure. A friend of mine once —

I think the bass could come right up in here, the man says and waves his arm at the plain of white-laced waves through the trees. The shad are out there, too, huh? he says.

I've seen them.

Okay, he says. Good luck. He moves off for the river bank. He turns his rod butt-first and begins a careful descent along an old rock piling that used to support the railroad tracks that once ran where we stood. You would think a smart fly rodder like that would have taken such a big rod encased piece-meal to the water if he had to sort his way through so many branches, but there this fellow goes with all fifteen feet of it.

I return to my innocent hatchery trout. After a short while I decide to move back up stream. I put my field jacket on, gather my stuff and move.

As I go up the path, I look down through the budding maples and tulip trees to spy on the two-handed-cast man. His rod is strung and he appears to be getting a streamer out of its plastic case. He stands on a rocky point just a few feet from the bases of the trees.

Directly in front of the man a fast channel, the point of a small, rocky island to his right. Beyond the tip of the island is a rolling plain of frothy water created by the rush from the dam. I expect he intends to wade out past the tip of the island and cast into the main river current. But that water is up and fast right where he is. I know for a fact because I tried to wade it the day before. I wonder how far away from the trees he has to go to be able to do his spey casting. With the slipperiness of the rocks, the force of the current, the wind, and the demands of that rod, it would be a feat if he were able to just stand out in a few feet of water and hold that rod up like a nylon Moses.

The shad are out there, though, and maybe a few early herring. There are muskie, too, and smallmouth and some big walleye. But if there is a striper out there right now big enough to make that giant fly rod worthwhile, shit, I'll drop my gear right here and take up tennis. No, golf.

I move on. I won't wait to see if two-hander catches anything. I don't like golf.

3.

My friend, Drew, and I set up along a stream in western Bucks County. There are supposed to be some big brown trout in this water.

We're both tired. The end of the semester, with its exams and parties, has taxed us. That is to say, we live cushy lives. The evening is warm. There is no wind. This is going to be very nice.

We have gotten here in the midst of the sulphur

hatch. We see some duns here and there. As I squat down to tie on a fly, Drew says to me, Have you ever seen a black man with a fly rod?

This is an unusual question, but as I think about it, I realize that in all the books, all the magazines, and on all the Tv shows, I have never once seen a black person casting a fly. Not once, ever.

I look across the stream to see why Drew asked. There, between the trees, is a wiry, short black fellow with some gray in his beard. He wears dark blue jeans, a green shirt, windbreaker, and a baseball cap. He has in his hands a thick, white rod set up with a fly reel. He studies the water.

I wonder about the rod the man has. It isn't a fly rod—its white fiberglass body is stout at the base and draws to a sharp tip like a teacher's classroom pointer—but I can see that it is fitted with snake guides, a wide stripping guide closest to the reel. I can also see that the rod is one piece, a little over six feet long. The reel is old, with solid silver sides and a double-armed wind. It is full of bright green line.

Drew and I finish setting up. We go in our hip waders down onto the gravely spit. We tread very light-ly, watching our shadows. The stream is about ten yards wide in most places; here, a tight, deep channel runs around the end of the spit toward the opposite bank and opens into a nice wide flat. Drew moves downstream.

The other fellow sees us for the first time and makes a face. I nod at him in greeting. He says, You guys are in my spot.

We won't be long, I tell him.

He shakes his head and walks downstream along the bank. He reaches a spot further down opposite from where Drew is. As I make casts I glance over at the blue cap sticking up out of the brush. The man is on steep bank that looks directly over the water. I can tell from his movements that he is setting up. Drew and I cast. We catch nothing. I wonder if the trout have had their fill of the sulphurs and are snoozing, bellies fat.

As Drew and I move down I tell him we should go past the place where the other fly fisher is. As we do, we watch him.

The man has eased himself down the bank and stands in about two feet of water in his sneakers and jeans. With a sideways roll cast of his right arm across his body he slashes out about twenty feet of line. He keeps it going in a sweeping arc in front of him, throwing the fly downstream with a roll and flick of his wrist, using the stiffness of the rod to direct the line. He lets the fly drop. The fly is large and black, and sits on top of the water when it lands. The man lets the current take the floating slack line.

The fly is moving by itself, giving little kicks. I tell Drew the guy is casting live crickets. Drew smiles, the sun lighting up his red hair. He says, That's just like Izaak Walton, isn't it?

Yeah, I say, you're right.

We see the cricket disappear in a swirl. The man reels vigorously, pulling the white rod hard against the line. He pulls the fish in close to himself, dipping his hand in the water and pulling it out by the gills. It is a nice brown, about fourteen inches. The man steps up the bank with the fish, unhooks it, and drops it in a steel fish bucket and puts back the lid.

Drew and I move to the next pool, stooped low and stepping very carefully in our hip boots. We make some good casts. Again nothing hits.

The man in the cap stops on the opposite bank, looks at us, and moves on with his rod and bucket. He goes downstream and crosses through thigh-deep water and moves up the bank where the stream turns left. We move down too.

In this bend there is a deep run that is a little fast then the water widens along some mulberry bushes, then flows into a nice flat. I see the man poke in his canvas bag of crickets and I say to Drew, Let's get down past him and cast just in front of those bushes. Something has got to happen.

Something does, before we get there. The other guy deftly slips down the bank and enters the water up to his waist without a sound. His footing set, he slings out his cricket, casting in the opposite direction than as before, but with the same arm and the same sideways style. The cricket plops and moves with the current until it drifts along the low mulberry branches. A dimple of water forms like a mouth below the bug and another trout has it. The man reels quickly, the thick rod breaking the fish, and he hoists another nice brown from the water.

Drew is amused. I am not. This fellow has beaten us to two holes and taken the biggest fish, perhaps the only fish in each spot. Does this man intend to move just abreast of us all day and snatch out fish with his crickets? I wonder if there is some fly fishing code of good manners that would require this guy in the baseball cap to offer to move back upstream to try the two pools where Drew and I failed while we move further downstream, hoping a change in the temperature and insect activity will raise the trout. But I do not know if there is such an unwritten rule. This is not a fly-only stream.

I step out into the current and walk a few paces until I am nearly opposite the man. He is up on the bank, squatting, head bent down over his fish bucket. The new brownie is clunking against the sides of the bucket. I say, Hey, there.

The cap comes up. The man regards me with squinting eyes.

I say, You're doing all right. What kind of rod is that?

Made it, he says.

I nod, saying, Oh.

The cap turns back down. He puts the lid on the bucket.

I say, Where're you from?

The man's head comes up quicker. He says, Allentown.

He's come as far as Drew and I have. I say, You going to keep moving downstream?

He looks from me to Drew then back to me. He says, Yeah.

I glance at Drew. I'm not sure if he is more amused by this man's success or by our predicament. I say to the guy on the bank, Look here, ah, you mind if we just walk ahead of you a bit so we all get some room to move?

The expression under the baseball cap is steely, the neck stiff. The man says, How about if I give you guys some crickets?

Drew giggles.

Give us a minute to fish this pool then we'll move further down, I say.

Fine, the man says. You ain't catching nothing.

We cast on the pool for a full ten minutes. Skunked, we move on.

Around the next bend we take out every fly box we have. I say to Drew, Got anything?

Got a brown hopper.

Me too.

We tie on the hoppers and start casting.

4.

I'm sitting at the counter at Sneddon's Luncheonette in town when this fellow walks in. I'm hunched over a big cup of tea. I waded all morning in the channel below the dam along the Jersey side and did not get a single small-mouth to hit the streamer. My legs are tired. This fellow sits down on a stool next to me.

I can see out of the corner of my eye that he is dressed Middle-aged Weekend Preppy, with khaki trousers, white shirt, red pullover, Weejuns, and a denim jacket with a corduroy collar. He also wears a khaki porkpie with a red-and-black tartan band. Set in this hat are many flies and streamers, so many the hat looks like an ice cream sandwich dipped in jimmies.

I put my cup up to my face even though it is too hot and pretend I'm deep in a big sip of tea. The fellow says, Hiya. I glance at him out the side of my eye and nod. He says, You been out fishing? I nod again. He looks me over. He says, I don't fish. But I like this town.

We're you from? I say.

Frenchtown.

You come all the way here to drink coffee?

I like the drive. I like to walk along the canal.

I nod. I'm telling myself, Don't do it—don't look at the bugger's hat or else you'll be here all morning.

I look at his hat.

He sees me. He says, You interested in fly fishing?

No, I say. Not really.

Best way to go, I think.

I thought you said you don't fish?

No, I don't.

Then why do you like fly fishing?

It's the most technical, he says. It requires the greatest touch. It's most artistic. What do you fish with?

Live ducklings.

The fellow guffaws but I can tell he's put out, and now he isn't going to quit. He takes his hat off his small, very round head and his wispy gray hair stands up in the static. He looks at me with a knowing stare from his bright brown eyes and his pale lips smile under his white moustache. He holds his hat on the tips of the fingers of his right hand. He pulls off a fly. He says, This one here is a Gray Ghost. Good for out in the river.

It looks like a little Christmas tree sprayed with fake snow on a hook, I tell him.

His head jerks back. Nawww, he says. It looks like a minnow.

I take a big sip of my tea, regretting that I ordered eggs and toast.

He puts the streamer back and plucks out a dry fly. This is a March Brown, he says. See here, this is how they're made. He holds the fly up between us like a coin he just pulled from behind my ear. He points with his free index finger, saying, This is the head. This is the hackle, very important part of a dry fly. It really makes the dry fly. And this is the tail. Do you know how a dry fly sits on the surface?

Surface tension? I say, finishing my tea. I see my breakfast coming.

Why, yes, surface tension that grips the hackle, he says.

I get my plate of eggs with four slices of perfect wheat toast. I ask for more tea and Rosemary, the plump, middle-aged woman who runs Sneddon's on weekends, takes the little steel pot, fills it with hot water, and puts in another tea bag.

Eggs aren't good for you, the old man says.

My doctor tells me to eat three a week.

He does?

My good cholesterol is down.

How come?

I'm a vegetarian.

A young man like you? How come? he says.

I can't stomach meat from a cow.

I thought vegetarians aren't supposed to eat eggs?

What kind of fly is that? I say and point.

Oh, that's a nymph, the fellow says and draws a big breath.

Oh, Jesus, I say to myself, that's the wrong thing to point at because you know what's coming now: the whole life-cycle story.

The man starts, You know what an aquatic insect is, right? Okay, well, they hatch out of the egg as nymphs and live underwater, underneath the rocks. They're like earwigs. Ever seen an earwig? All right. When they get ready to metamorphose they rise to the surface where they crawl out of their old skin and —

Are you talking about those big green bugs with the pincers?

Ah—what? No, those are praying mantises.

Is that one there supposed to be a praying mantis?

No. That's supposed to be a Green Drake. Don't you see it looks like a fly, not a praying mantis?

I eat more eggs, sip some tea. I watch the man as he mentally regroups to get back into the saga of the insects. I say through a mouthful of egg, What kind of machine makes them?

The man stammers then says, Machine?

What is it, like a sewing machine or something that wraps all that stuff around them?

The fellow grows pale and his eyes glaze over for a minute. He looks around the room and puffs his cheeks then faces me again. He says, My god, you can't make these on a machine. They're made by *hand*. Hours of painstaking work.

I crunch a bite of toast with marmalade, chew, and wash it down with tea. I wipe my mouth with a paper napkin. I look at this bugger and say, You mean to tell me that someone takes the time to sit there and wrap all that stuff onto a perfectly good hook so it looks like some kind of insect?

It's an art, he says, raising his head with a stretch of his neck. He plonks the hat next to my plate as evidence.

I look at the hat. I say, They don't look like bugs to me, man. They look like fake bugs. Those bugs you see in those trick ice cubes look more real than this.

He shakes his head sharply. It doesn't matter what you think, he says. It's what the fish believes these flies look like that matters.

I point at a Royal Coachman and say, Well, what do you think a trout thinks this one looks like? I stuff eggs in my mouth.

The man says, That appears like a very bright, very edible sort of mayfly to a trout.

What's it called?

It's called a Royal Coachman, he says, as if he named it himself.

I swallow my eggs then gulp some tea. A Royal Coachman? I say.

The man is turning red.

I point to a small salmon fly and say, What's this one called? Her Majesty's Blue Booby?

The man half steps off his stool on one foot. He grabs up his hat, clenching it. He says, Young man, you have no appreciation for the greatest flies ever made and I hope you spend the rest of your life with your worms and salmon eggs.

As he comes to his feet, putting the porkpie back on his head, he says, And the service in here stinks.

The bugger skulks out letting the screen door slam and he shuts hard the outer door. A few heads come up then turn away uninterested.

I look at Rosemary and smile. I say, Thanks.

She never offered to take the man's order.

5.

A woman walks into the Orvis store at Madison and 45th. She is maybe 30, maybe older. She is dressed casually but nicely, the perfect Upper East Side WASP woman's look: white linen shirt, unbuttoned down to her collar bone, tucked in a very smooth tan skirt that ends midthigh, and a gleaming red-brown crocodile purse she carries like a football. I don't have my glasses on but I think her eyes are green. She stands just in the entrance and looks around for a minute. From where I stand at the second floor balcony, looking through the spread of display rods, I can tell that everyone in the store who can see her is looking at her.

She looks up and sees the rods out in the air like giant cat whiskers and goes up the stair past the front register. She is tall but moves with a dancer's precision. She has long wheat-brown hair flowing over her neck. Her neck is long.

I put down the Silver Label rod I'm contemplating and wait where I stand. The woman moves along the armory of rods, reading the label beneath each where its butt is cradled in the wooden frame.

Women who fish are far and few between. Female fly fishers are even more rare, and stylish, interesting ones not wearing wedding bands are more rare than the rarest Western trout. I watch her pick up a long eight-

or nine-weight. She jiggles it in her hands.

The compact, lean Italian-looking store clerk who had talked to me moments before comes up behind the woman, says, Hello, and asks her if he can help her. She says she is going fishing for salmon. The clerk politely and succinctly tells her about the heavy, fast rods in front of her, recommending a couple of them. She nods, smiles, says, Okay She picks one up in her hands. The clerks says, Feel free to check them out, see which one feels right. Let me know if you have questions. Then he smiles at her and saunters away. He knows he may or may not have a sale with me, but if he plays it right he's got nearly a guarantee buy with the woman: she doesn't know what she should get, she may not have ever fly fished before, and if he tells her just enough to get started, as he has, bides his time and let's her fill with more questions, then comes back and really goes into detail, she'll buy the rod he recommends. I like the guys in this shop because they're smart and nice and would not do anyone a wrong turn ever, but they've got to sell stuff.

The woman picks up one of the rods. I watch her body move underneath her shirt. Why should I like her? I don't know. I don't know her but I like her. I pick up a rod in my hands and let it wobble ever so slightly until it tips the end of her rod.

I say, Oh, I'm sorry.

She looks at me and smiles.

I smile. I say, Where are you going to fish for salmon?

I may be going to Scotland, she says, looking at the rod in her hands. Her head moves very precisely, bird-like.

Have you ever caught salmon before?

She shakes her head.

They're well worth the trip. I caught salmon in

upstate New York and they're just...great, I say, my voice slowing when I can see I'm going to get nowhere.

She studies the rod. She says, Mmmm.

A motion below catches my eye and I see a man coming up the stair. He is tall and in good shape. He has a tanned, florid face, a thick orange-haired moustache combed neatly, and thick orange hair around the sides and back of his head, the top bald and tanned. He wears a very nice blue chalk-striped suit, white shirt, and shiny gold tie. He comes round the top of the stair like a retriever let loose and he picks up the nearest rod, a fantastic aught-weight on the very end. He holds it in his hands and makes the tip lash. He says to the woman, Think that'll do?

I can tell she smiles at him even though her head is turned.

He says, What do you fish for? He speaks loudly.

She says, Salmon.

Oh, great fish. I've caught some upstate. Alaska's next. Where are you going?

I may have to go to Scotland on business. I thought I'd do some fishing.

Scotland. Mmmm. Let's see. He ushers himself into her and without touching her with his hands guides her a few feet as she moves in response to his movement. They come within a few feet of me. The moustached man picks up a stout nine weight. Looking at the rod, then at her as he speaks he says, This is what you want. Power Matrix. Nine weight. Pretty good all around. You can use shooting lines with this. I have. See, he says, picking up another rod, this one is one size down. Take it in your hand. Now hold this one.

I watch this man jiggle the rods then put them in the woman's hands. Feel that? he says. She says she does. For the life of me I cannot figure out how you could tell the difference between jiggling a nine-weight and jiggling an eight-weight, as if jiggling a fly rod tells you much at all.

I move back down to the Silver Label I was looking at. I want it. I hold it in my hands as I listen to this fellow tell the white-and-gold woman the better points of the rod he says she should buy. He starts talking about Sage rods, then custom-made rods. He says, Look, why don't you come with me to the river I go to and we'll take a whole bunch of rods and you can use them and find out what you like. I've got all this stuff. Light weights, salmon rods.

The woman presents the right amount of polite suspicion, saying, And your name is?

Eric. And at least don't buy this rod yet. Let's go to this place I know on Broadway where they make rods. We could look at a few different things there.

You really know this well.

Of course. Been doing it since I was fifteen. Come on, I've got a car.

The woman puts down the two rods she was holding, looks back into the shop to say thank you to the clerk, then goes down the stair with the man who starts talking loudly about the salmon in Scotland. He has his right arm across the small of her back, again guiding her with a cushion of air.

I go to where they were and hold the eight-weight in my right hand, the nine in my left, and waggle them ever so slightly. I shrug. I put them back. I pick up the Silver Label again and turn to the clerk. He walks over.

I say, Don't you just hate guys like that?

Yeah, the clerk says. I had that sale.

6.

In a nice, easy-wading eddy at the Water Gap I cast a cone-head Muddler. It's already eleven in the morning but I keep fishing because the night before in the same spot a very good fish hit and I got it close enough to see it then it was off. It was about fifteen inches maybe. I don't think it would hit this time of day, but you gravitate toward good places, hopeful.

Just above me is a rush of water around a bend with some white ruffles here and there. Kayakers have been running up and down this stretch for the past hour. I don't pay them much attention until one of them sweeps into my pool with an easy turn of his hull and sits himself just within range of my casts.

I am tying on a bigger cone-head when I look up and see the purple kayak and the fellow in his black and green propylene jersey and blue helmet. He is looking past me to the riffles above, over my right shoulder.

I finish tying the knot and look at him. He looks at me. I look at him as if I expect him to say something. He looks at me as if he expects me to say something. I say, Ah, you're kinda close.

I'm just waiting for my friends, he says.

You have to wait for them right here?

He says, They'll be here in a sec. He shrugs

I tip my hat up a little bit. This guy looks like the sort of guy who would be pictured on the cover of a trendy outdoors magazine: he's got the gear, he's got good teeth, he looks a little like Pete Sampras, the tennis player. I start stripping line off the reel.

I remember when I was a teenager a friend and I used to go shooting at a farm outside Hackettstown. We used to shoot M-14s, civilian models that were semi-automatics. A yellow dog that lived on the farm liked to come out with us and invariably sat out near the water-filled beer cans, or laid himself down right in front of us. The dog had no memory yet was gun shy, so before every shooting session came the moment when we said, Time to shoot the dog, and we lit up a few cans near where he lay or shot right over his back, and he would yelp and run away and leave us room for bad shots and ricochets.

So I get the streamer moving, make a false cast to my right, bring it back and load up a fat cast. As I'm doing this I'm watching Kayak Man's eyes following the tuft of streamer on the end of the line. I lay the rod out a little high, and the line lashes outward, unfurls, and the streamer comes around like a tiny mace and dings the fellow in the helmet. He startles and shouts.

Whoops, I say, loud enough for him to hear me. The streamer fell in the river and I strip it in and begin loading another cast. It's not that I don't like kayakers—they're fine, when they're polite.

Don't you cast at me again, Kayak Man says.

You parked right in the fish, I shout.

It's a big river, he says. You gotta cast right here?

I sling the line and put the streamer over his bow. The fellow makes a mean face at me and starts out with a surge into the current, going back up river.

It pays to have a good cast.

TEN

The Solunar Life

There had been little snow, so the river did not rise in the early spring, and the water was not as cold as usual. The shad run, then, may have come early, because the shad move up river as the water warms. But they had not come. Not one appeared even as the first spring moon waned.

Pete was not interested. He didn't like shad because he disliked their illegitimate strike. He reasoned that a fish truly hooked, fought, and landed had struck in the first place because it preyed upon his fly; it attacked, and did not simply bat something out of the way and become inadvertently hooked when it had no plans to eat.

With this essential predator-prey tenet unensured by shad fishing, Pete was unconcerned that the shad had not reached town. As he ambled to the pizza shop on the corner, or down to the Acme, people grumbled about the shad being late. He said nothing to them because he had nothing to say, except that shad tasted awful and just weren't worth a damn. He was a lean, short man with buzz-cut iron-gray hair and horn-rimmed glasses. He knew no one would pay attention to him because he was short and wore glasses. People did not notice his strong gray-blue eyes in his rugged face, nor notice the easy stride with which he walked. Had they noticed his keenness, they may have asked his opinion. He would have told them that the fish were attached to rhythms, as all things were. They would suddenly show up in surging droves, quickly passing the town en masse. That would be that. Pete himself did not understand the rhythms and currents of his own life, but lived by them.

Last year the shad run came and went, passing him by while he was drunk. He never got drunk as badly as he had these past two years. He had always had jobs with regular hours. If a man didn't want to lose his job, he fought it off or somehow limited his drunks. Also, an electrician drunk on the job who confusedly touched a live wire burst into a white flame so hot that the man's teeth, bones, and tools were the only things left in the pile of ash, and Pete did not want to die that way.

But when he came to town he became part of a contracting business and worked jobs on and off as a foreman. Because he wasn't touching wire as much, booze was closer to him than ever. He had come to town because of a woman, and perhaps the booze was connected to her somehow too.

So in this usually warm spring, he felt the drunk coming on. He didn't mind. He knew it was coming. There was no booze in the house. He would get some, when the time came. Fishing, as it always had, was holding off the drunk. He was fly fishing on the South Branch and the Pequest, and he drove way up to the river above Calicoon, catching trout there. The early season had been dull, the trout very tough to take. He had caught one good brookie out of the Raritan, a fish that had survived from a stocking several years earlier and turned wild: it's colors were bright—its blue-dotted sides and crimson fins—and its lower jaw had curved a bit. He let the fish go.

In the winter, a terrible dread clung to him after he was drunk. He was drunk twice, long, during the winter. When he was sober and bored, he felt indifferent. There was not much electrical contracting to be done in the winter. When he was soon to get drunk, that was when he began to want to do something outrageous and irrational. Then he was drunk, and then done with it, and was left with only himself and a tired loathing.

Not that Pete was evil, or dreadful, or awful to work with. He was worst when he was alone, except when he was fishing. When he was fishing, he was grand. When he wasn't fishing, he was mostly alone. Though it did not have to be that way, but it was. When he thought hatefully and did not think of himself, he thought of a man named Walton Godwin.

Pete had fished for Walton Godwin. He caught fish for the man and gave them to him. Pete did so for one reason: to be around Walton Godwin's wife as much as possible. He was in love with Betty Godwin.

He had seen her several times in a grocery store, in Carlisle, Pennsylvania, where he had once lived. He knew with one glance down the long canned goods aisle that she was married. When he got closer he also saw that she was not entirely happy—something in her big green eyes was not alive enough for a woman who still had a love in life, womanly love, not mother's love. But what could Pete have said to her? *You look sad, and I'm a little sad too, and maybe we could go see a sad movie and then sit in the car for a while?*

Pete said, M'dam, excuse me, do I need watercress for egg salad?

She looked at him. Her eyes mocked him a little. She said, No. You need eggs.

Pete managed to get himself invited to the Memorial Day picnic at the woman's house. This was not long after the War and a tremendous sociability had taken over people's manners so that married women in a small town were not afraid to invite polite strangers to parties at their home.

So that weekend Pete drove to a big yellow house in the middle of a wide field. He met Betty's tall, heavy bodied, auburn-haired husband, Walton, who shook Pete's hand with a body-shaking pump and patted a heavy hand on Pete's shoulder. Pete intensely disliked bigger men touching him that way—patting his back or clubbing a fist down lightly on his lean shoulder.

Amid the big crowd of people, Pete ate very good food, tried to remember people's names, and watched everywhere Betty went. He watched her introduce her three-year-old son to several women who mooed over the boy and kissed him.

Eventually Walton Godwin cornered Pete while the latter sat on the porch slowly drinking a third beer. Pete never got drunk around others, though he arrived drunk numerous times.

The big man said, Eating good?

Pete nodded.

Were you in the service?

Yeah. I was in the army.

During the war?

No. I was discharged in thirty-six.

Oh, Walton said, nodding his big head. I was in Washington, he said.

Combat unit? Pete said intentionally.

Hell, no. General staff.

Pete nodded. He guessed Walton Godwin was his age, 33. He supposed Betty was about 25.

Pete, I hear you're a fisherman?

Yeah. That's right.

What do you fish with?

Flies.

Oh, you're a fly fisherman? Walton said. Mmm, that's good. Listen, Pete, I've got a proposition for you. I'm running for mayor, and I need to get some press. You think you could maybe catch me a few trout. I want to have a picture taken for the paper.

Don't you have time to fish? Pete said.

Well, you see, I don't. I really wish I did, but between meetings and the boy and all, well, I'm not a carefree bachelor like you. Hell, that's probably why you're not married, all that time fishing when you should be going in to town—the big man laughed loudly at himself.

Pete swirled a gob of spit in his mouth and looked at the front of the man's shirt.

Walton Godwin stopped laughing and said, I'll give you ten bucks for a couple trout. If you can get them by tomorrow afternoon, call me and I'll get them from you.

Pete took a long swallow of beer. He said, I think a largemouth bass would be right for you.

Why?

More mayor like, I think.

Can you get two? I want to have more than one.

I can, Pete said, watching the profile of Betty drift by out the corner of his eye.

All right then, Walton said and braced Pete's shoulder with his hand as if trying to loosen a board.

That night, Pete went to a farm pond and pulled out two four-pound largemouth on a big popper, two good fish, and cursed himself for taking them. He put them in his refrigerator then took them to Walton the next day. He called ahead and Walton told Pete to meet him in a field down the road from his house a few hours later. While he waited to go, Pete wasn't sure if he was going to keep from drinking too much to drive because the current in his body was changing and it was time he drank. He went for a walk. He didn't smoke so he chewed stalks of buckthorn. Then he drove to meet the man he caught fish for, feeling like a sinner and a smuggler, about to tell the man he would never do this again.

After the exchange of bass for cash Walton Godwin invited Pete back to the house for a beer. Pete would have gotten his own beer, but he did not pass up a chance to see Betty. When they pulled up in the driveway of the big yellow house, Pete saw Betty standing on the gravel holding the boy. Looking at her he feared his life was over.

Walton Godwin got out and boomed at his wife and son, Come here, and grabbed the small boy out of her arms and jogged around the side of the house, shaking the boy in his arms.

Pete walked up to Betty. She looked at him. He was short enough that he looked straight into her eyes. He told her how nice she looked. She blushed. The red on her face made his skin warm.

How was fishing? she said.

Pete didn't want to lie. He said, Walton's got two nice bass in his creel. He went to Walton's car and took out the creel. He followed Betty into the kitchen.

Pete sat with Walton on the back porch and listened to the man tell him about being in Washington D.C. during the War and how he should have stayed there. They drank beer and ate sandwiches that Betty made. It was all nearly too awful for Pete: being around Betty, and not being drunk.

A friend of Walton's arrived with a camera to take the picture for the paper. He took a test shot of Walton sitting in the chair, holding up one of the bass. Then Walton sat on the short stair to the lawn, held up both fish, and smiled.

When it was over, Walton offered Pete another $10 bill as they stood in the driveway. Pete stared at the money in the man's big hands.

It'll cover you for next time, Walton said.

What?

Catch me some more.

What for?

Just in case. I might have a reputation I got to keep up now. I should have some fish on hand just in case someone asks.

Pete thought this was the most insolent thing he had ever heard. Then he took the $10, put his hat on, and walked to his car, the '30 Ford he bought when lived down South.

As whispers of, *No shad,* went around the town, Pete cleaned his reels and took a fine cloth to his rods, which were all bamboo, and cleaned them off gently. He began to feel better. He made some calls and got some work—supervising for the contractor, odd jobs, consulting on county projects—then spent two weeks doing steady work, not drinking at all. He fished whenever he had time.

Everyone in town gave up on the shad. The editor of the newspaper made calls to the Fish & Game Commission and was told that no one on the river had seen shad anywhere. Pollution was blamed and fingers were pointed at the Philadelphia shipyard. The Lewis Island fishery pulled in channel catfish and big carp in its haul seine. A load of frozen shad was shipped from the Chesapeake for the annual shad dinner at the firehouse.

Pete laughed when he read in the paper that frozen

shad were coming to town. Maybe frozen shad were better because the cold killed the taste. He went from his cluttered living room to his cluttered den where he checked the solunar chart for the month. The new moon was two nights away. The air was warm. He gripped his face with both hands, sweating his own internal rhythm. He could do it, he decided. He had a beer, just one, and thought of Betty and how he could have been married to her right then and there, possibly for two or three years already. He stopped thinking about it because it was worse torture than ignoring drink.

Pete had been married once, when he was 20 and just out of the army. He had been stationed at Fort Jackson, in Columbia, South Carolina, and had met a woman five years older, who was divorced, and had a young son. Her name was Pat. They married and lived together for less than a year. His wife told him he had made a mistake marrying her, saying he had married too young. For a while after she told him this, he spent his nights sitting on the porch, drinking beer. He had never been bothered so much by the heat before and drank very cold beer until he couldn't hold any more. He had never been drunk before that.

One morning his wife asked him if he was going to leave. He said he was. She said, You see, I was right. I shouldn't have agreed to marry you. I want you to leave before Earl gets too used to you.

Earl was her son, who was seven. The boy was not visibly wrong but lived in a world all his own and did not talk. Pete's attempts to play with the boy were haphazard.

Pete resigned from the job he had with the telephone company. He had been trained as an electrician in the army and pole climbing for the telephone company was decent work. One day after work he packed his two bags and left a note for Pat. He said he was sorry that he had made a mistake; he felt terrible but his poorly written words said clearly none of how badly he felt nor told exactly how responsible he knew he was. He left his forwarding address in case she needed money, though he left her half his savings.

He moved back to Maryland and lived with his older brother for a while. When the divorce papers arrived, he was startled and greatly upset that the marriage was not annulled instead because there really was nothing to call for as strong an act as a divorce. He hated himself for not knowing enough not to ask the woman to marry him, and for not finding out how to get an annulment. He figured that if he left, the marriage was annulled because they hadn't been together for long. He felt bitterly stupid and naive. He was a boy who had wanted a woman and thought he had to be married to have one. He vowed never to repeat such a mistake and put the signed papers in the mail.

Then he went fly fishing again. He had learned to fly fish as a boy on the Shenandoah. He stopped when he was in high school and did none in the army. Alone, living in an attic in his brother's house, fishing suddenly seemed like it was all he was going have.

The best fish Pete ever caught was a smallmouth bass on the Susquehanna River. The fish was maybe four pounds and though was probably not the heaviest smallmouth ever caught on the river, it surely had to be one of the most glorious. That was the summer of 1949. The reason he caught the fish was that at the time he was still fishing for Walton Godwin, and this tainted terribly a beautiful success, though he hoped that the true glory of his battle with the creature, and how well he and the fish both fought, raised him above the charade he had foolishly joined and the harm done to a woman that he participated in.

That June evening the fish struck soon after Pete cast the streamer and let it drift just past the edge of froth overtop a submerged rock. The smallmouth ran with a long dash when Pete set the hook, taking line off the old Hardy reel. Pete kept the rod bowed, turning his arms and the rod to stretch the belly of slack when the fish turned or leapt.

The fish ran in an arc with the current, jumping here and there to create a path of foam like a lightning bolt fading across the surface of the water. Pete's chest filled with the hot air pumped out by his heart, surrounding his heart in a hot bubble of exhaust. He focused all of his mind onto that fish. He felt the fish's turns and holds. The strength of the fish filled his hands. The jolts of its turns and dives snapped like rope ends in his forearms. He focused so hard on the fish and felt it so keenly in his hands, he believed he was running like a bolt of electrified flesh down the line to the fish, matching every one of its moves with a twist or shrug of his fluid body.

As he got the smallmouth closer, into the stage of the fight when everything becomes brutal, hand to hand, Pete crouched over the water that turned a darker and darker blue as the sky darkened. He felt himself pulled down to the water, his nose inches from the surface. The air around him liquefied and turned blue. The edge of water and air blurred. He took a few steps sidewards, his movements slow under the weight of the water on his legs. He heard the river, the fish, and nothing else. The sound of the river was quiet and cottony in his ears. The sounds of the big smallmouth on the surface were the only loud sounds, and were exactly the same as a man's hand swept in and out of the water as if trying to uncover layers of current.

Pete breathed the water that evaporated off the surface. He breathed steadily, feeling purely alive.

He held out the net. Over the wooden edge of the net was a flash of gold. It disappeared, then reappeared. With learned grace Pete's body automatically stretched and twisted just enough, just so, one arm sent just a little bit higher, the other sent further, a half-inch expansion of muscle and bone that crossed the immeasurable dimension between air and water, angler and fish—and then, fully stretched, the gold came forward and slipped over the edge of the net. Pete shifted a foot forward and nearly slipped under. Water lapped the edge of his waders. He looked down into the net. The great small-mouth lay in the mesh as if born there.

Pete's heart slowed. He began to understand that he had fought such a grand fish successfully. This fish should have broken the leader, thrown the hook, or wound the line around his legs and jerked him under.

Then his heart began pounding and he was able to hear again. He let out one short, high-pitched whoop then tucked the rod in his waders. He turned the net into the current so the water washed over the fish's mouth, then he reached down into the net and put his index finger into the fish's mouth, his thumb under its jaw, and he turned its mouth open. The Mickey Finn was hooked in the corner of its mouth. With his pliers Pete plucked the streamer out.

He held the fish in the net, then let the net fall back on its cord and he took the big fish in both hands. Its sides were olive-gold, tiger-striped with bronze, its belly ivory, its eye ruby red. No fish had fought Pete with all its strength and skill as this one had. Committing its image and weight to memory he put the smallmouth back into the water and he held it there, his fingers holding its mouth open, as the rush of current moved over its gills. He looked at the fish through the water, and the fish looked back with its intense dark eyes as if it intended to attack Pete no matter how much bigger he was.

Finally, the big smallie began to tug its head. Pete held it from underneath. It flexed its body. He tapped its side and it bolted.

He rose up, water streaming from his chest and hands. He saw the last moment of sun.

Walton Godwin asked for more fish, whatever Pete could bring him, for $10 a trip. Walton met Pete somewhere, on a country road or a back lot, and paid for the fish, but did not ask him back to the house, which was all Pete wanted out of the exchange. Pete hoped for a chance at being alone with Betty to try to do something to let her know how he thought about her. He didn't care if it was an adulterous thing because she was too lovely to pass up. He had lived alone long enough to know. He was not a soldier boy doing an impetuous thing.

He never saw photographs of Walton Godwin in the paper with the fish, and all of his campaign photographs were of him in a suit waving both hands. What the hell was he doing with the fish? Finally, one afternoon when they met at an old warehouse, Pete said, What do you need these fish for?

You never know when you need extra, Walton said. My wife likes to cook.

Why aren't you fishing?

I go out, but I haven't got much luck.

Do you fly fish?

Some, the man said, his face maintaining its usual extra glee.

Do you know what a Peck's Popper is?

A popper.

Who makes it?

Peck's.

What's Peck's full name? Pete said.

I don't know, John Peck maybe.

Pete took a step forward. It's Peckinpaugh, you dope.
Now what the hell am I giving you fish for?

Walton squared his shoulders and looked down at
Pete. He said, Look, I pay you for these fish. You're
compensated for your time.

Yeah, well, my time is up.

So you're saying you don't want to get paid to fish
anymore? Walton said, his tone mocking. You don't
want to get paid to do something you like to do?

That's why a man doesn't get paid to do it, Pete said,
almost spitting as he walked back to his Ford. He realized what he had been a part of.

On the nights he guessed Walton Godwin was not
home, Pete parked his car off the road near the man's
house, sat there in a colonnade of tall spruce, and
watched the light in the windows of the house.
Sometimes Betty moved past one of them. He wondered
what she thought about while she waited for her husband
to come home from fishing. He wondered what she
would do if he got out of the car, went up to the door,
went in, and told her how he had dreamed of kissing her
white cheeks and her closed green eyes, of putting his
arm around her middle to hold her tight to him.

What about my son? What about him?

She would only ask such a complicated question if
she seriously considered leaving her husband. She was,
Pete understood, a dedicated wife who suspected her
husband all along but saw no alternative to being faith-
ful. He remembered his own mistakes, from years
before, when he was too young to really be called a man
though he had been married.

He realized, sitting drunk in his Ford, in the dark under the trees, that he had what people called "a past." Married women with children do not leave their faithless husbands for uneducated electricians with a past.

A loathing welled in him. He was a short, bespectacled, drunk divorced man. He put the car in gear and wove his way home.

Walton Godwin lost the race for mayor. He and Pete never saw each other again. Pete sometimes saw Betty downtown in Carlisle. He never went near her.

Walton Godwin was stricken with polio in 1956. He died a year later. Pete felt very badly for Betty, and for her son. When she decided to move away, he was sunk. He visited her and said to her, You could find a smaller house, closer to town. But she shook her head. She said she wanted to make a clean start. She moved to a town in New Jersey and lived with a sister for a year, then found a home in a nearby town and bought it. Pete stayed in touch with her, and went to see her twice. Both times he asked if he may see her again. She said, I like seeing you, Pete, you know that. Of course, this was no admission of desire.

On impulse, as impulsively as he had joined the army at 17, or gotten married, or moved from his brother's home to Carlisle, he found a small house to buy in Lambertville. He packed up his small bungalow in Carlisle and left, quitting his job, not missing many people. He missed how close he had been to the Susquehanna, and the good trout streams, but after he moved he had the Delaware, the Raritan and its South Branch, the Pequest, and a day's driving to the Upper Delaware, and the streams of eastern Pennsylvania. Not a bad exchange.

Of course, there was Betty too. He knew he moved to try to have a chance with her.

He was careful to call her on the telephone before he visited, and he made sure he did not ever show himself to the boy, whose name was Franklin, and who was often at a cousin's house or playing baseball. He remembered guiltily his own legal son, and also felt a clamminess because he had known Betty's son's father and was now trying to woo that man's widow.

Pete was not a success. He and Betty went on a series of dates each year until Pete allowed his intentions to give over to seriousness; to trying to kiss Betty forcefully and thoroughly and say he loved her. She became cagey. Their summer ended. Maybe he would see her at Christmas. Then he called her in the spring. And again from May to August they would meet for lunch, or dinner, go to a movie, or sit together on her porch. Every year the same thing happened.

This warm spring, he was not going to call her, he was not going to go by her house. If he did, he knew he would ask her out again, and ask her to marry him again. And then what would there be left for him to do? Moving directly to the bourbon was much neater.

He remembered how her house looked, the living room all finished wood, the curtains white lace. He remembered the last time he had seen her, a year earlier; he sat on the sofa and ate cake and drank coffee with her.

He said, Betty, you know how much I like you.

I know, Pete, she said.

I'm in love with you.

When he said this she ducked her chin and glanced at the floor. Her hands were folded on her knee. He put his hand over her hands and said it again—I'm in love with you.

Pete, she said, I don't know what to say.

I'm just asking if we could go steady.

The woman's shoulders slumped. She agreed to see him some more. He took her out twice for dinner, one time taking her to a cinema all the way in Flemington. That night when he parked his car in her driveway, he said, You seem like a sleepwalker.

She smiled and shrugged. I'm just thinking about my son, she said.

Why?

Because he's in the National Guard now.

Oh, yeah, Pete said. He'll be fine.

They won't send him overseas?

No. Not Guardsmen.

Isn't the National Guard part of the Army? she said.

It is, but Guardsmen stay home.

Betty nodded. She looked out the window. Pete shook his head slowly, to himself. He reached over, grabbed Betty's arm, pulled her to him and kissed her a long time. She did not pull away. She did not kiss him back. When he let her go, she looked at him blankly. He got out of the car, opened her door, helped her out, walked her to her front door and there kissed her again. This time she pushed her head forward but her lips were still. As he walked back down the steps he said, Betty, you can do what you want. He's been dead ten years now.

I know.

Then it's me, huh? You don't like me.

The woman held her purse in front of her. She swayed a moment, distracted, looking at the steps. She said, Pete, it's going to be a long time before I love someone again, the way I think it should be.

You think it can't be right with me?

I don't know, she said.

Pete buttoned his jacket. He said, Betty, I'm fifty-one. You're forty-three. Patience is not a virtue for us.

She looked at him sourly for a moment. She said, You make it sound like I should settle because I'm getting old. She was still very beautiful and Pete recalled that was how she appeared the first time he saw her, how she spoke, carried herself and looked at him were still all the same.

We can't act like we have the world at our feet, and we don't have to act like we know nothing about what we want, Pete said. We don't have to act like we don't know what men and women want. He felt himself sway a bit with the candor of his words. He was completely sober and always was with Betty.

Betty heaved an impatient breath. She said, Maybe I just don't want any of it, Pete. Maybe one marriage was enough.

Pete looked at her a moment. He decided there was nothing to say to make her love him. He said, Goodnight, and walked back to his car. He drove to his home. He got drunk and stayed drunk for two weeks, two hot, hard weeks without eating much, missing work, sitting in the same clothes and drinking. When it was over, he studied his living room to recollect, if possible, the time he had spent intoxicated. He always wondered at the fact that when he was drunk, he didn't smash any chairs or punch the walls no matter his frustration. The worst he did was throw a bottle toward the kitchen when he finished it. He saw some broken glass—brown and clear, beer and whiskey. He sobered up on apple juice, pancakes, eggs, and turkey sandwiches.

He planned to walk into the river a few days later, but decided the river wasn't right. He made it through the summer dry. The fishing was good. Winter was hell. Then it was spring again, and the shad had not appeared.

His face seemed weary and pale as he looked at himself in the mirror when he shaved the night before a fishing trip. His nose was getting blotchy. He realized that in June he would turn 52. He wondered how much money he had. He wasn't able to pay attention to his own thoughts. He looked over his bank papers but was unable to read the numbers. He turned on a stronger light. The numbers were indecipherable on the page. He was tired from long hours on a job.

When he awoke very early, he did not feel that he was able to move. His body had turned to clay. Worse was the return of the terrible feeling, a heavy, fearful strain. He usually felt this long after he drank. Now it had flipped over on him, though he still felt like getting drunk. He felt worse than that. He became fully awake. It was four a.m. He got up.

He dressed around six, then sat in a chair. He felt something corrupted about himself that he had not felt before. For certain, today had arrived like an unknown season. He nodded to himself, his head fuzzy. If he had to die, himself, by himself, then that was that.

By nine o'clock he went out the door. He did not feel like staying in his house. The rooms were stuffy. He went down the street. His walk was slower, but had the same ambling jounce. He knew, because he was short, that short people have a more forceful walk—less body to move across less space, but relatively the same amount of power that a big person had, if not more. This thought helped him a bit, a last bright idea about himself. He carried it with him, thinking that if he had married Betty, they would have matched nicely for photographs. His body in a suit would not have dominated hers in its dress.

He went into town, across Bridge Street, and further along the canal. He looked at the buildings and shops.

He wondered what day it was. A Saturday, yes. The sky was low with gray clouds.

He walked along the railroad tracks. He felt the ties under his feet. He waited for them to hum. He kept going. No hum arose through his feet. He looked back. He did not see the wavering ovoid shape with its bright dot in the distance, a diesel coming his way. He looked South and saw nothing but a channel of green and brown: no train. He shrugged. He had all day. He would find a train or it would find him. He wished he was drunk. He wished he had written a note so that his brother's son got his fly rods, but he hoped the boy would get them anyway.

Pete arrived at the wing dam. He looked down. The length of the cement wing showed a dusty brown in the morning light. Bushes grew in the debris that had been stacked up against the top edge of the dam. The thing looked like a big sandbar. Pete scaled down the bank and went out on the cement. He was amazed how a simple spit of concrete altered a very big river. He walked all the way to the rounded end that was edged with old brick and looked out at the frothing water that rose as if it were alive. He remembered watching big American shad bullet through the current and gleam momentarily like silver spearheads then disappear. That was his first spring in town, not that long ago. Nothing had changed since then.

He turned and walked past the water coursing fast along the bottom edge of the dam to the turn-around near shore, where it went south again and flowed through a channel between shore and a small island. He stepped off the dam and moved over the rocks to the shore, the tips of his boots touching the very edge of grainy silt and water. He was amazed no one was around, not a single person casting a line.

As Pete crept along the trees began to lighten. He looked up. The last edge of clouds scudded by and the sun's brightness from over the hills behind Pete changed everything. The sky was a bright blue. He was unmoved, and did not turn around. When he got to the end of the channel, to where it opened in a pool and rejoined the river, he saw that this was where he must decide: go into the river, or wait on the tracks.

The brightness of the water startled him. He thought the sun and waves created the brightness.

Then he saw them, thousands and thousands of them—shad, rising and cutting the surface with their cleaver-edged backs, their silvery sides reflecting rainbows of sunlight. They came like a huge pile of treasure, all silver and precious gems, poured in a slough from a trove. Disks of light reached Pete's eyes from the millions of coin-sized scales. The water was beautifully alive with the shad; the fishes' thrashes and surges changed the sound and image of the river.

Pete was awe-struck. A strong, pleasant sensation slowly filled him, then quickened and shook him like voltage. He believed he felt himself plunging head-first, his body spinning circles in the swirl of the water and collective body of fish, the water gurgling in his throat and ears as he blew bubbles. He was subsumed.

He shook where he stood. His eyes filled with flashes of light as his gazed upon the plain of silver fish. He coughed, thinking he breathed water.

The fish continued past, the big American shad flashing quickly beside or atop the layer of hickory shad that comprised the main of the procession. For every four or five smaller backs that shone, a big, broad, darker back flashed among them, the slab sides of the American shad creating a flash that outshone for just a second the bright bodies of the smaller fish.

Pete looked up, his eyes shot with black, white, and orange flashes. He imagined how the long procession appeared from the sky; surely, it was like a big circuit board, signals coming in and going off, lighting an indecipherable signal.

Pete moved up and down the bank, watching the shad make their way. He saw where the procession began, coming off the middle of the races and taking its gleam as it moved into shallower water then gaining the pool at the bottom of the channel. He went back to the dam and watched the fish wrap through the turnaround and force themselves into the mad swirls off the end of the dam. There they disappeared, driving down and under to move through the fast water. Somehow they found slips of water between long blasts of current and drove upstream with sharp shakes of their tails. Pete saw them go by just under the first crest of the rapids. Beyond that, the shad had a wide, easy plain of water to rest in before they moved on. He did not see them out there. The water was green and unbroken.

Pete stood on the dam looking back down over the fast water. He imagined the procession in his head: a glorious flow of color and light. He had not expected to see such an amazing thing. It made him feel ashamed to think he had considered throwing himself in the river, a dead body an ugly sight amid the brilliant, life-driving shad.

When he got back to the center of town he was out of breath though he had not gone fast. He gave up on telling anyone what he saw before he even tried. Someone else would see the shad and word would go out. He realized that the shad had waited until the strong signal of a new moon and sun pulling on the

Earth sent them on their way. He counted back five days, the day of the new moon, and guessed that was the day they moved out of the bay and started upriver.

Inside his house he plunked in his chair. What a thing he had seen. He was sure he had seen it, a great wave of shad, fish he refused to catch. He laughed at himself. He felt odd.

He read his bank statement and saw he had enough money for a mortgage payment. So he wrote the bank a check. He looked at the calendar. He thought that in five days he would go up to the West Branch. Then he got drunk, just a little drunk, enough to last for a little while, and he let himself think of Betty before he told himself he shouldn't think of her. That was all right because then he was drunk. He mumbled a song to himself, wondering if ever anything he did was going to make a difference. The day darkened into a warm spring night. He began tying flies in the light of his desk lamp.

ELEVEN

The Grand Slam

Uncle Seamus sat with Len on the patio, under the umbrella. They relaxed on chaise lounges. Seamus was quiet for a long time. Len looked askance at him. The man appeared to be remembering something. The sun was very bright and Len squinted at the reflections off the bright leaves of the rose bushes nearby. The whole property, with all its trees and bushes, was a chessboard of solid shadow and gleaming wedges of sunlit green. Len didn't wear sunglasses because Seamus didn't like people wearing sunglasses; the dark, goggly eyes confused him and he shouted, Look at me, when people in sunglasses looked at him.

Seamus was hoping for a grand slam as good or better than the one he had last week, or yesterday, whichever day. He drew his breath slowly and said slowly, People sometimes weren't sure the snook should have been a part of the grand slam, you know?

They should be, Seamus, Len said. Snook, that is.

Seamus looked over his shoulder and down the long lawn to the hedge. His gaze wandered, slightly unclear, over the hedge to the woods beyond. Well, he said, the weather looks good.

Where'd you catch the snook, Uncle Seamus?

Seamus shook his head irritably then looked squarely

at Len. Yeah, snook. Some people thought snook shouldn't be part.

Len said, How many snook yesterday?

Um, three. Then the tarpon, Seamus said. That tarpon was good.

I'll bet, Len said, sipping lemonade. Any permit?

There's a secret to them.

What's the secret?

Seamus held his clenched hands up against his chest and nodded, then slowly returned his hands to his lap. The gesture was setting the hook.

Len smiled at his uncle but Seamus didn't smile back. He blinked at Len, somewhat fazed. Len said, What's the secret?

Seamus looked down at his hands where they rested. They did not seem to him that they were his hands; though he felt their weight, the flesh seemed dense and insensitive. Len asked again about the secret and Seamus had to think before he spoke, saying, It's the hands.

Len nodded. He leaned back and closed his eyes. He was glad everyone else was gone: his sister, Leigh, his mother, Peg, Aunt Janine, who was Seamus's sister, and both Seamus's daughters, Kelly and Beth. They had all gone shopping. Every time one of them had come out to check on Seamus throughout the morning, they put their hands on his shoulders and stood behind him, as if to push him out of the chaise, or sat very close and leaned into his face as if to measure the light in his cataracted eyes. They talked to the old man in queries and polite cautions when he spouted off about something. Len hated to watch it.

Len's mother had called him at school before the end of the semester. She said that Uncle Seamus was "starting to slip" and that if Len wanted to talk with him while he was lucid he should come home for a visit. Len said he needed five days for exams and then he could get away.

Seamus was Len's favorite great uncle, favorite only in that he had been the one to give him his first 12-weight rod, a big heavy Sage. His other uncles and great uncles had all set fine examples, given him good things and a lot of advice. But when Len was too bashful to ask his father for such an expensive piece of equipment that he would rarely use, and did not have the cash on hand, Seamus somehow sensed his nephew's want and delivered the goods as a college graduation present. That uncanny sense Seamus once had about wants, those of people and fish, was now swallowed and divided by his problematic mind.

When Seamus began fly casting around the gardens and trees, Len's mother, Peg, again called her son at school. Len was turning in grades, handing in his own papers, and wondering how to make it through without a summer assistantship when she called. She said, Len, come home for a little while and see Seamus.

Is he worse?

Yes. He wants to go fishing.

Well, let him.

He wants to go to Florida.

Put him on an airplane then. Send one of his daughters with him.

Len, don't be insipid, please. Uncle Seamus can't go anywhere.

Len held his breath a moment. He said, You're not going to put him in a home, are you?

His mother said, I think between myself, Aunt Janine, and either Kelly or Beth, we can keep him here for a while, but eventually we'll have to move him to either Kelly's or Beth's and get home care, I think.

Why is he at our house? Not that it bothers me that he's there.

It's closest to his. It's just a stop over. They have to decide who's going to take him in.

Why not his sister?

She's getting old too.

But Aunt Janine said she'd take him, didn't she?

Yes, she did, and she's only two years younger than Seamus. It would be too much for her.

Len shrugged when he hung up the phone. The next day he put his rent check in the mail and got in his truck. He drove the scenic route through North Carolina and Virginia, and managed to stay awake to cross half of the very long state of Pennsylvania. He arrived at his childhood home in the boonies by midnight. Everyone was in bed. His father was away on business. The house was utterly silent and made Len mindful that somewhere in the dark was a very weary, heavy head.

Len looked at the old man. Seamus had lost most of his grey-brown hair and large, thick freckles covered his head. His face was tan and leathery, his eyebrows shaggy. His hazel eyes were discolored by the cataracts but still intense, darker than they once were. The most sure indication of his state was that he was dressed simply and a bit disheveledly, for Seamus in his day had been a sharp, precise dresser and had reached the point in his fifties when he had enough money to have several tailored suits and numerous tailored shirts. In front of Len he wore a gray sweat-shirt half tucked into worn-out khakis, and flip-flops. His unshaven face looked wrong.

Len had awakened that morning to distant shouts and as he wandered into the livingroom he looked out the big bay window to see his mother, Aunt Janine, and cousin Kelly standing around the old man who was blathering and shaking his fist. His right hand held an old fiberglass 12 weight fitted with a big black Pflueger reel. Seamus's back cast of a tarpon fly caught in a huge blue spruce too high to reach with the rod tip. He jangled the line, shouted curses, and was in a fretful state.

Len wandered down the lawn in his bathrobe, went up to Seamus, and said, Hello, Seamus. Snagged?

Seamus turned with a start, began to turn away, then recognized Len and said, Hey. It's a good day, then bellowed, Goddamn it!

Len brought the ladder, plucked the big Apte fly off the pine bough, and tossed it down. Kelly and Len's mother coaxed Seamus up to the patio and sat him down. They talked him into breakfast and he acquiesced because he was hungry.

As Len poured himself coffee in the kitchen, his sister, Leigh, came in. What was Seamus doing? she said.

Fishing, Len said.

He was doing that yesterday and the day before.

Where?

Here. Across the lawns. Old Mister Waylan led him back yesterday afternoon. We went crazy looking for him. I don't know how he does it, Len, but you'll turn your back and he'll be gone. He's like a ghost.

What did Waylan say?

Seamus was casting at Mister Waylan's bushes, she said. Then he shouted at Mister Waylan to get out of the water.

Len laughed.

Why did mom bring him here? Leigh whispered.

She's trying to preserve the peace during negotiations.

No one wants him, huh? Poor old widower.

Aunt Janine will get him, which I think is right. She

wants him with her.

Such a burden.

All she has to do is put a fly rod in his hands and he'll be fine.

You're nuts like him, Leigh said, and went back to her room with a banana.

After breakfast, Len sat with Seamus in the shade of the umbrella. His mother asked if he would watch the old man for the day because, she said, everyone needed a break. He watched all the women leave en masse. He waved them off as they drove away, then sat back and sighed.

Looking at his uncle, he guessed that this was the way he would go himself, this or cancer. Senility and cancer were the family killers. Those sicknesses had ended the lives of his grandparents and some of their many siblings. Len was down to two great uncles and three great aunts, all in their seventies. He did not know if he preferred cancer or senility. He had seen senility in its last stages with a few other relatives and he wondered if its mental storm was worse than the bodily wracking of the *Big C*, as his own father called it.

Come on, Seamus, we're going fishing, Len said.

The old man said nothing. Len repeated himself until Seamus said, Where?

We'll go over to the South Branch.

South Key?

The Raritan, Seamus. South Branch. The Gorge.

Key West, Seamus said. Get a boat. The Marquesas.

We'll go there later. Let's get in some trout.

Seamus shook his head. Braddy, he said, you know I hate trout. "Braddy" was Bradley, Len's father.

Since when do you hate trout?

Since the first grand slam, Seamus said.

Len smiled to himself. He remembered that Seamus

had a grand slam back in the late seventies when Len himself was a young boy. Seamus must have had a few more around the neighborhood, casting to forsythia and patches of ivy.

Seamus said, It's not that long a boat ride from here, Braddy. We can make it.

When should we go?

Now, Seamus said with urgency.

Len would have put old furniture around the back-yard and let Seamus blast the settees and chairs with a .12-gauge if the old man asked for it. As a matter of fact, that sounded pretty good, and there was an attic full of furniture. But how could he find a way to get to the Marquesas?

Seamus whispered to himself. Then he turned and looked at his grand nephew, his eyes cloudy but focused on Len. Yes? he said expectingly.

Do you know where you are, Seamus? Are we in the Keys? Len asked sincerely, and with sincere curiosity, because he did not want to invent a charade the old man did not already possess himself.

Seamus said, Are we?

Len considered what he wanted to say. He wanted to entertain Seamus, and give him some emotional adventure; not hurt him or make a monkey out of him. He rubbed his temples. He said, Are there fish out there, Seamus? He pointed to the huge front lawn. Along that bank? Do you see fish? Tell me if you do.

Seamus peered into the distance. Slowly he nodded. I see 'em, he said. Tarpon. They're swimming on the other side of that bank. Seamus pointed to the very edge of the property where stood a long pile of mulberry bushes. Len went to his room and found some old flies, then went back outside and took the old 12-weight from where his mother had hidden it in the garage. He tied a ratty old Cockroach to the heavy leader then handed the rod to Seamus and said, I'll get the wagon.

Seamus faced the far mulberry bushes, his face wan but his eyes locked on the spot where the tarpon's dark backs showed. He nodded.

Len went around the back of the house. He hoped to give Seamus a nice morning of casting, and was pleased to find what he wanted—a battered wooden flatbed wagon mounted on a heavy chassis with big lawn mower tires. It had been used years before by one of the caretakers before the adjoining properties were sold to real estate developers. It was still used for hauling away leaves in the autumn. Len grabbed the handle on the end of the steel arm and pulled it out of the tall grass and drove it around the corner of the house. The wagon wasn't hard to drive backwards by pushing and steering with the heavy arm.

Halfway around the house, Len stopped. He wanted to know if this was wrong. No one was there to tell him if it was or wasn't. Was it patronizing to indulge the fantasy of someone half out of his mind? Then, stubbornly, he shoved the wagon along. Sometimes in life all one has is fantasy.

Seamus was standing on the edge of the flagstones as Len approached and when he saw his nephew he caught his breath and pointed. His hand trembled slightly at the end of his long arm. Len helped Seamus into the wagon. Seamus crouched unsteadily on one knee and held the side panel with both hands. The big rod stuck over the front panel. Len pushed the wagon from behind, going slowly, the fat tires sinking into the thick grass as they went until they were about sixty feet off the end of the bushes. Len held the wagon, standing on the grass below Seamus. Seamus breathed hoarsely and said, There are two big ones. Just coming onto the edge, see?

In the crystal green water, two thick, bluish bars angled against the grain of the water.

The wind's with you, Len said.

Seamus rested against the wooden panel, legs aside like a soldier fallen after a long march. The long rod wagged with vibration. Seamus said nothing. He faced the water ahead. The tarpon there lolled at the surface, their silver scales turning the water to opal around them. Seamus watched the brown fly sail and snap with a false cast and he flexed his arm just as the rod loaded.

Len looked to where Seamus looked. He saw the black dots of big bees that moved among the thick branches of the bushes and shoved themselves into the flowers, entering and wriggling with ecstasy. Robins called in the distance.

A tarpon swallowed the fly and Seamus's entire body stiffened when he saw the huge dark hole of its open mouth. He waited, letting the fish pull back and turn a few feet, then struck, bouncing where he sat, setting the hook. He let out a gout of breath as the big tarpon exploded out of the water and flung itself through the air. He cupped his line hand, cinching it until the line shot through with minimal burn. His arms jerked. There was little line to clear and soon the tarpon was on the reel. Seamus let out a happy groan and held on. The fish jumped again and Seamus strained to bow with the rod. The fish's violence felt as if it would pull his body off like a glove, leaving him sitting with just his mind in the boat. The tarpon leapt a third time and threw the hook. It was a lovely fish. Seamus smiled.

Len said, Seamus? The old man hadn't moved.

Seamus looked at the young man and smiled.

Still see them? Len said.

Seamus nodded. Len rolled Seamus down the lawn a short distance. Here Seamus cast to a lone tarpon lolling next to a grass bank. This one wasn't as big, maybe 30 pounds. The fish nosed into the fly and Seamus let it drift, sink, then gave it an expert twitch that did not pull it away. The tarpon turned at an angle to the fly, its big eye studying the prey. Seamus twitched it again and pulled it an inch and the tarpon turned and gobbled the fly. The fish came forward to deeper water, its mouth closing, the water rushing out its gills, the fly sandwiched against its upper plate. Seamus stripped slack madly then set the hook with a hard whip of the rod. The fish leapt forward, clear of the water, ran past the bow, and the reel sang.

Len watched the old man hold both hands to his chest, his mouth open. Len looked out where the tarpon ran away from the bank toward open water. Seamus turned to Len with wide eyes. Len got behind the wagon and pushed.

The tarpon made four great runs and ran Seamus into his backing. He slowly gained line as the boat motored over the widening, deeper water. The fish changed direction, turning toward a further flat. He fought the fish with his heart as much as his arms, back, and legs. His heart pounded against the pounding heartbeat coming across the line. When that heart slackened his did not, the pleasure and excitement driving his pulse as he brought the fish beside the boat.

He held the rod over his head and looked down at the long, lovely fish, the fly sticking out of its mouth. Braddy reached down and had the fish by the tail and pulled it over the gunwale. Flashes of sun off its scales filled Seamus's eyes. He laid back.

When he opened his eyes and saw where he was, he said, That way, and pointed. His arm was aimed at the pines near the road. Len said, Woman Key? The Marquesas? He pictured a map in his head.

Seamus talked to himself, whispering the words and thinking them over before he said, Yes. The Marquesas. He thought to himself: At the Marquesas there might be permit. No, there must be permit there.

Len pushed the wagon past the dogwoods and Japanese maples. Jays screeched in the upper boughs lit by the hot sun. Len went through the pines, over the shallow ditch and past the big blue mailbox. He looked right then left, then crossed the quiet road. The wagon bounced over the other ditch and down a mowed trail between the old forest and a field of planted pines.

Seamus watched the pelicans come out of the distance and sail by. He watched the water. The boat shot over turtle grass that gave way to deeper water. He didn't know how he was there or for how long, but he had caught and let go one good fish and felt that there had to be more. When he looked ahead the sun lit the water and the far key seemed to be elongated like some kind of mirage. The water browned. He thought his eyes were troubled and that he had been burned by the sun. He held his breath a moment, unsure that the boat was right. He felt as if he were being dragged bodily through the water. He closed his eyes and held his hand over his mouth. He thought about how a permit appeared when it noticed a fly, how it turned and nosed in. The way it held its body and whether it stiffened its fins or not told if it would take. Then there was the way to strike them, a sure strip-strike that should not be too soft but could yank the fly out of the permit's mouth if done too hard. He was not able to remember if Braddy was with him or not when he hooked and lost a permit many years ago.

Len envisioned the edge of Woman Key in the line of beech trees at the bottom of a small mown field ahead. He turned the wagon to move with the grain of the mown grass and pushed Seamus slowly. Len shouted, See any?

Seamus saw that they were moving with the outgoing tide. He looked back at Braddy and gave him a strange look because he crouched by the motor. The young man was not doing much sighting at all. Get up, Seamus said. They both stood in the boat. Seamus wiped the sweat out of his eyes with his shirt, felt his head and cursed because his hat had blown off. He put his bandanna on his head. He looked out along the expanse of sand-bottomed flat that extended southwesterly off the key.

Len thought he saw something—a blackbird feather? a vulture feather waving in the grass?

Seamus saw it too and quickly bent to the fly box and found a nice Nasty Charlie. He took up the rod and tied the fly to the leader. He pointed and nodded, trying to force the words out his dry mouth. He said, Where's the rod? Which one am I using?

Len said, You've got it. Right there. Where are they? Just there. Three bones. See?

Where the dark fingers waved in the green-olive flat were the bonefish, the edges of their tails sticking up in the sunlit ridges of water.

Seamus rose to cast. For the first time, he had the rod in his hands, so Len sat on Seamus's left. The wagon was stable enough that it did not lurch on its axles as Seamus's body motion set up a big false cast then rocked off his feet a bit as he went back then forward with the intended cast. The black feather blew up in the breeze. Seamus huffed because the bones had jumped forward as his cast unrolled so the fly fell behind them. He let it go down and jerked it a few times. He did not see the fly but he saw the top of the leader and he twitched the line with his stripping hand so the pink gleam of sunlight on the leader slid up and back. One of the bones turned, then the other two did, their bodies level.

The interested bonefish advanced. Seamus pulled the line easily but smartly then stopped. The bone tailed. Seamus pulled again and the bonefish pecked, pecked again and pounded the fly then turned to the side. He did not know if the fish had the fly. He carefully stripped six inches of line and struck with the rod. A star of green-gold exploded on the surface and out of that came the fly shooting toward the boat until it slowed and fell.

Seamus huffed with disappointment. He sat down. The fly line was strewn on the field.

Reel up and we'll go further down the flat, Len said.

Seamus sat still, looking at the trees. Len reached over and squeezed his uncle's hand. Seamus stared at his nephew then looked down at his hands. He saw the line and reeled it back, then took off the bandanna, wiped his face, and tied the bandanna clumsily on his head again. Len shoved the wagon along.

Further down the line of beech trees were more bonefish. Seamus said clearly, Bones, when he saw them and Len stopped pushing and looked where Seamus pointed with the rod. The rod was like a vector on a chart, a shiny brown line that led to the few odd-angled, darker lines that were bonefish in the clear, greeny water. Seamus was connected to them, feeling himself like a line drawn with one motion of a pen down the rod, over the line, to the fish. He wasn't afraid of the sensation, his body, vision, and mind cinched and fitted so his chest and hips and legs bent—he slipped through and out his right arm so he went down the rod and was sliding down the line to the fish. He was directly over them, their bodies heavy gray lines amid the glitter of the water. Seamus hovered happily in thin air.

A bonefish turned on its side, its big eye looking up at the man's face, the fly stuck in its jaw. Seamus braced himself with his arms, forcing himself back down the rod, feeling his legs fitting through the bottom of the rod, his insteps bouncing over the cork handle. He was back in the boat, the rod part of his arms and ribs, and he pulled on the weight of the bonefish. He had this one hooked. It dashed through the flat.

Len sat with Seamus in the wagon as his uncle gripped the side panel, his arms shuddering now and then and he lowered and raised his torso, his jaw jutting. The bonefish was making a big run. Len looked out where the fish was and wondered how it felt and how hard it pulled. He waited until Seamus looked directly over the side of the wagon. He knelt beside his uncle, reached down, and pulled in all the loose line until he had the Nasty Charlie in his hand. Seamus looked at him, his eyebrows hooded over his eyes, his mouth slack. Suddenly he put his head back, his eyebrows raised to reveal his eyes and for the first time Seamus appeared to know just what he had done. He said, Good one.

Len smiled. How many bonefish have you caught, Seamus, ever? Did you keep track? Len said.

Seamus looked at Len and said, Braddy, is this your boat?

Yes, Seamus, he said. What do you think of that sky?

The old man squinted at his nephew, shaping some unspoken utterance, then caught sight of Len's finger pointing skyward. He looked up. The sky was hazy but the sun shone through brightly. Seamus said, Let's go.

Len spun the wagon around and hoped that Seamus had no map in his head and did not know which way west was, or else Seamus realized that Len had just driven the boat into and over the mangrove. Seamus made no protest. Len pushed the wagon along the line of beech trees then broke through them to another field and went along an old tractor lane. He was going north.

Seamus watched the water go by as they crossed the Boca Grande channel. A group of frigate birds flew away in the distance like a handful of black sparks drifting in the air. The channel was calm and the wind was near dead, coming in sighs from the west. Way up in the sky were pinkish white clouds like gooey cotton candy that oozed out of the haze. Seamus thought about his house and the fields where he lived.

When Len got to the base of the small hill ahead he skirted it, aiming for a stand of tulip trees. He went through the trees to a wooden fence. Here was the border of a horse farm. It used to be a regular farm, but thoroughbreds had replaced corn and cows. Len ran along the fence until he came to the corner and went through the saplings there then into a wide circular clearing, a thick woods of sumac, beech, and tulip ahead.

Len imagined that this was a lagoon in the interior of the Marquesas. He stepped up into the wagon and said, All right, Seamus, we're here.

Look at all those frigate birds, Seamus said.

Len watched the tops of the distant trees swish in the breeze. A storm was building.

We're in the lower part of the Marquesas, Seamus. Let's try up along the edge here. Len pointed at the trees on his right.

Seamus sat up and looked around. A beautiful, wide circular pool extended before him, the water green, then azure, then blue as the light changed the water with distance. Alongside and from beyond, he heard the rustle of the mangroves and smelled the broken-leaf odor that carried in the air. The breeze came now and then, very slight, from the west; good for a right-hander.

They did not go far when Seamus raised his hand,

catching his breath. In maybe four feet of water directly in front of the boat were three big motes tipped with black: permit. Seamus stripped line, looked again at the fish and rose to cast. The Nasty Charlie hit the water and the fish disappeared. Seamus sighed. He stripped in the fly, held it in his hand, and watched the water.

Len watched his uncle leaning over the front panel of the wagon, staring at the long grass. The old man had not yet touched the rod. Len pushed the wagon slowly. The breeze was dying and the humidity rising.

Seamus turned and crept back to Len. He nodded and wheezed, putting his face in his nephew's face. He said, There are permit all over this flat. I'm going to get one.

I'll keep my eyes peeled, Len said.

Seamus turned and took the rod in his hands. He looked at the fly at the end of the line, the Nasty Charlie, and looked around for the other rod. He said, Where's the other rod? He did not understand what Braddy said in reply. He no longer wondered why Braddy wasn't helping sight more fish, because obviously the boy was no good at it. Seamus squinted at the water as his nephew poled along. When he again saw shapes tipped with black quills, he raised his hand and gave a low grunt. There they were, at ten o'clock, two permit as big as welcome mats. Seamus cast the fly to them and it landed too far away. He tried again and the lead fish flared its fins and the two of them raced off. Seamus watched them go, wondering how such bright silver animals were capable of disappearing so quickly in clear water.

The afternoon dragged on this way. As Len moved all around the edge of the clearing, Seamus spotted permit, cast to them, and either missed or flushed them. Once Seamus was so exasperated he let go the rod with a jerk and seethed through gritted teeth. Len wondered if permit populated the Marquesas like this, and if Seamus had been there once when they had; or if they were swimming in some flat in Seamus's mind, along some ideal, absolute key west of everything.

Len got in the wagon and said, What's going wrong?

Seamus looked at him and shook his head.

What aren't we getting it right?

Seamus studied his hands. Whatever was wrong with him was centered in his hands because they were heavier than he had ever known them to be. When he cast he was unable to have just enough touch to match the power of his stroke, and when he stripped the line, he pulled without crispness or delicacy. He had been fine for the tarpon and the bonefish, but now, wearying under the sun and effort to cast, a leaden fluid filled his hands. The fluid was in his shoulders too, and behind his eyes.

He looked at Braddy. Damned permit, he said.

What's the secret? Is there something you're forgetting to do?

He did not know what Braddy meant. There was no secret to permit, none that Seamus knew. If there was, it was the secret that the fish kept itself, for when it did like your fly, it gave no high sign. The fish simply swam over, dipped, and ate it. Beyond that, there had to be the excellent draw of the stripping hand coordinated with the rod hand. Yet the motion was no secret; it was simply a very fine physical act not easily entered or completed, like bending a note on a guitar.

Seamus said, It's wrong. In my hands.

Let's try a little more. We can't give up, Len said.

You cast for a while, Seamus said. He sat in the stern of the wagon, hands in his lap, staring blankly.

Len stood with the rod. He picked out a few spots along the edge of the trees, a root here or twig there, and cast to them. He managed eighty feet pretty well. He was happy to be casting in Seamus's secret key, wondering what it was about permit that was so impossible.

After half an hour's practice, Len looked at the sky. A pile of brown-grey sat in the west. He looked at his watch: 3:30. He figured his mother, cousins, and great aunt were by then in an immeasurable tizzy because he and Seamus were gone, without leaving a note. Len had not expected the trip to the Marquesas would take so long.

He looked around and realized they had made a whole circuit of the clearing. He pushed the wagon and the catatonic Seamus back to the entrance, near the trees. He knelt next to Seamus and pointed down the tree line. Seamus, he said. I see one. A nice permit, just there.

Seamus shifted and craned his neck. I don't see 'em.

Watch. Just beyond the dark patch.

Seamus watched the water for several minutes. Yes, he said to himself. His breath hissed over his lips. Yes, yes, yes.

Len watched his uncle lean over the panel, face forward, straining.

Seamus made the cast. The fly landed just ahead of the fish, the permit facing the fly. Seamus saw the fly as it sank. The permit rushed over, halted, then tipped its head down, tail up. Tension came through the line and rod. Seamus waited an extra second then moved both hands apart, and the line came taut in his hand, the rod bowed. He took a deep, uneasy breath as the permit ran fast directly away from the boat. He got the fish on the reel and the line sizzled away until the fish stopped abruptly.

Seamus wound the reel madly for a moment, then pulled back on the rod. The fish was still there. It seemed to kick the line a few times before it ran side-long to the boat, far out into the middle of the flat. Seamus moved along the edge of boat, rod up, squeez-ing his hands reflexively to keep a sense of touch in them because he was afraid they would go completely dead and he would have to fight the fish without any feel at all.

Seamus knelt in the middle of the wagon. Len said nothing. He braced the wagon from the front so it did not roll as Seamus moved.

The permit was just into the backing. Seamus slowly wound the reel and pumped the rod, fighting the fish through vigorous turns of its wide body as it attempted further runs. It made a dash this way, then went further, sat, then went away into the middle of the big flat. It pulled hardily and sprinted this way, then that. This was a fine fish. Slowly, Seamus brought it back. He whis-pered, Just leader. Just close enough.

The permit was on the surface twenty feet away. It broke through the water then dove. Seamus wound it up again. He looked at the tip top. He had maybe ten turns of the reel to go before he got to the leader.

The permit made a strong dive and then turned in a wide arc. As the old man turned the rod to follow the run his hands seized. He was unable to grip the reel knurl and his rod hand feebly clenched the handle. He moaned and spat, his left hand tapping at the side of the reel. He hooked his index finger on the knurl and tried to jerk the spool around. The permit nosed down hard and buzzed away from the boat, and the rod bowed in his hand then began slipping away. He wrapped the rod with his other forearm and fell forward on the gunwale, trying to trap the rod. Where was Braddy? He sensed the young man moving behind him and he tried to lift himself off the rod so Braddy could grab it.

As Seamus got to his knees and pulled the rod high, he looked at its bowed, quivering shape. He was so upset, so disgusted. Braddy did not take the rod from him. The permit did not stop running. God did not help him. With all he had left in his hands he held the rod handle and pulled in an attempt to turn the fish.

The line gave without any loud twang, and the rod went soft. Seamus reeled clumsily, furiously until he found the cut end of the leader. The permit had finned it.

Seamus groaned, *Oh*, so loudly Len asked if he was all right. The old man bowed down in the wagon, his face in the crook of his elbow.

Len panicked for a moment. He cried his uncle's name then pulled the old man's arms until he turned Seamus over and rested him on his back. Seamus's eyes were open but doped. Beads of sweat and tears ran off his face. His sweatshirt was stained dark across his chest.

Len said, Seamus, can't you hear me? He took Seamus's pulse. We'll go home now. It's going to rain.

Seamus said nothing.

Len pulled the wagon as fast as he could back up the slope along the horse pasture, back to the narrow, mown lane and then up past the pine tree field to the road. They went up the front lawn and around the side to the patio. Len picked Seamus up and pulled him over the side and walked him into the house. When everyone in the kitchen saw them coming in, and saw Seamus appearing so wrung-out and ludicrous with his red bandanna on his head, they immediately separated uncle from nephew.

Len weathered a blistering round of questions and harangues from his mother and great aunt over Seamus's absence. While Len sat in the livingroom, cornered, Seamus sat in the kitchen, forlorn and tired, as his daughters rubbed wet, cool cloths over his face and arms. His horror at the loss of the permit was not diverted by a large piece of pie put before him by Leigh. He did not want to eat. The fish was still with him but was gone.

After the storm came through and cleared the humidity and heat, Len sat in the living room in the dark. The electricity had been knocked out, but not the telephone. He sat in the lamp light drinking a beer and talking to his father on the telephone.

He calls me Braddy, Len said.

Mmm, that's understandable, his father said. But please don't run off with him again. Neither one of us needs to get another earful from your mother or anyone else.

Do you know what the secret to permit is, dad?

Don't go after them and you won't suffer.

Seamus said he knew the secret of catching permit.

I doubt that.

Did Seamus ever have more than one grand slam? Len said.

Who said he had a grand slam?

He did, himself.

Len's father sniffed. He said, One time while I was down there with your mother's parents, Seamus went out and caught a bonefish, then a small tarpon, and then all he took were snook the rest of the day. I don't think he ever seriously fished for permit.

He was talking about snook today, Len said.

When did he say he had a grand slam?

Today.

Well, today wasn't his best day, was it?

He never said to you that he had a slam? Len said.

I don't ever remember, and that's something you wouldn't forget, his father said.

Maybe he was explaining it once to me when I was a kid and I thought he'd actually done it.

Memory plays tricks.

Yes, it does.

They said goodnight and hung up. Len rubbed the cold, wet beer bottle on his cheeks then wiped his face with his hand. He leaned back and said, Damn, wondering what terrible things he had forced upon his uncle.

Asleep in another room, Seamus dreamt of putting his heavy hands in the bright water to saturate them, and draw out the corrosive fluid. Then his blood took its saltiness from the sea and flowed freely again in his hands. The sense of touch returned to his fingers and palms. He felt the line between his fingers as lightly as if touching his wife's hair.